A RISK WORTH TAKING

Meg and her father run a public house by the sea, but Pa is also involved in the 'night business' — helping the smugglers evade the excise men. More than anything, Meg wishes he could get out of the gang's clutches; but when Pa brings home an injured man to hide in their attic, it seems the family will be more involved than ever . . .

ALYSON HILBOURNE

A RISK WORTH TAKING

Complete and Unabridged

LINFORD
Leicester

First published in Great Britain in 2024 by
D.C. Thomson & Co. Ltd.
Dundee

First Linford Edition
published 2025
by arrangement with
the author and
D.C. Thomson & Co. Ltd.
Dundee

*A catalogue record for this book is available
from the British Library.*

ISBN 978–1–4448–5461–9

1

'Oh, Pa,' Meg mutters, and turns over for the umpteenth time, pulling the scratchy blanket with her. 'Where are you?'

He tells her it is a risk worth taking but Meg can't sleep on the nights her father is out on a smuggling run, not until she hears the Alehouse door creak and his footstep on the stair, meaning he is safely returned.

She lies on her straw pallet, one eye on the worn shutters, gauging the time by the wraith-like streaks of light appearing through the cracks, indicating approaching dawn.

She and Pa have argued many times over whether the night business is worth it.

'The money —' her father argues.

'We can survive with the Ale house. We could grow more of our own vegetables and get more goats,' Meg says.

'I'm a brewer, not a farmer,' her father

grumbles. 'And besides, the night business is more profitable.'

'Until you get caught.' But Meg doesn't say it loudly enough for Pa to hear.

An owl hoots outside, making Meg jump. She lifts her head but there is nothing more.

She shivers as she thinks through the dangers.

Whatever money her father may earn in the night business, it is not invested in the Alehouse. The thatch is mossy and thinning, and on wet, stormy nights Meg can hear water dripping into the attic above her bedroom.

The wattle and daub between the wooden wall braces of the upstairs needs work and the treads on the staircase need replacing, as do the stools in the bar and shutters on the windows.

The Anchor is in desperate need of repair.

Pa's only weakness is a fondness for a fine waistcoat. Twice a year he orders a new one to be made, in fine silk or dusky velveteen, often with an intricate pattern.

'More difficult to see the stains,' Pa says, rubbing at a newly made mark on his latest purchase.

Meg gives him a tense smile. It doesn't matter that he wears a heavy leather apron for brewing.

Running an Alehouse involves slops of beers, smuts and singes from the fire, spatters and drips of fat from serving meals and clearing plates, to say nothing of the oil lamps and candle lanterns that need constant trimming and filling.

And meanwhile, each time Josiah puts out a call, her father leaves, spending his night unloading barrels of Hollands, French brandy, bundles of cloth and lace, packets of tobacco and boxes of tea from the ships that bring them across the Channel from France and Holland.

The booty is stacked into carts and barrows and secreted away to hiding places across the county, and Meg has another disturbed night wondering if her father will return or whether he'll be on his way to the assizes in the morning.

For safety, the landing places change

with each delivery of contraband and can be up to twenty miles away. On these nights Pa isn't home until daylight and Meg remains sleepless, too.

Next to her, her faithful, mixed breed, mud-brown hound, Jip, twitches in his sleep as a rabbit squeals in the marshy fields beyond the dyke, an unearthly cry that sets Meg's nerves on edge.

She has no doubt it has been caught by the fox that prowls the rough grassland, a wily, tatty creature, its patchy fur the colour of new conkers. It has been taunting her hens for years and only her constant nagging at Pa to fix their pen keeps them safe.

When Pa is not here the night has an extra silence. Meg misses his gentle wheezing snore and the creaking as he turns in the night. His presence keeps other sounds at bay.

Sounds like the mice crawling through the spaces in the ceiling above and the floorboards beneath her. Their movements whisper through the building and Meg shudders, unable to unravel words but sure the message is for her.

For a moment she imagines the Ale-house is full of ghosts, and a chill makes the hairs stand on the back of her neck.

It doesn't matter how small she makes herself, the murmurs continue to swirl around her, poking like sharp fingers. Meg turns, pushing the woollen blanket away and wriggles on her straw pallet, but despite being dead tired she is still awake.

Eventually, unable to stand it any longer, she rises and goes to the window to open the shutters.

It is still too dark to see much but the sound of waves lapping on the mud flats of the estuary drifts through the small glass panes.

She is tempted to go out and walk down to the water's edge, but she knows she'll regret that decision in the morning when it is time to rise.

Instead, she stands, staring out into the blackness, twisting her thick blonde hair into a single plait that hangs down her back. Her hair is too heavy to be kept in place by a few hair pins and she is too busy in the Alehouse to spend hours curling it or trying to make it look elegant.

The Alehouse stands at the end of the dyke that runs along the river's edge, near where the river empties itself in the sea.

The business relies on trade from the sailing ships that pull in at the staithes to unload, ready for smaller boats to take the goods up the river to the town.

The sailors, longshoremen, boat hands and local labourers call in for lunch and dinner, sure of a hearty meal and mug of ale to keep them going. The large, rusting anchor set in the ground outside the Alehouse has given the place its name.

Meg rolls her shoulders, knowing that soon she will have to go and stoke the fires, knead and set the dough to rise for the day's bread, and put on a pot of stew. The chickens will be squawking to be let out and the goat will need to be fed.

It is unfair of her father to put her through this. He should be back by now, surely.

Her body is tense. She cannot relax.

As a child, she dreamed of escaping the Alehouse, but since her mother's death when Meg was twelve, she has slipped into the role of landlady, and now her father would find it hard to cope without her.

For a while, she hoped he might remarry, and someone might take over her mother's role, but there are no widows in the village, apart from Mistress Cooper, who is not the marrying kind.

And Meg has to admit, as much as she loves him, Pa doesn't have much to offer a younger wife, apart from years of hard work.

He is round-shouldered and stooped, but still strong enough to lift barrels and sacks of grains, which is why Josiah keeps him on as a tubsman to shift the contraband from the boat to the carts that carry to hiding places.

Something creaks and Meg freezes, holding her breath, but then nothing follows, and she realises it is just the cottage settling itself down, like an old lady shifting her petticoats to be comfortable.

She should be used to the building's groans by now but at night the sounds are louder and more intense.

A curlew whistles outside and makes her jump. Meg clenches her teeth, and when she turns and she can see her shifts hanging like a ghostly figure from the hook on the wall, so she knows dawn approaches.

She listens, straining to hear footsteps coming along the dyke or on the stair as Pa tries not to wake her. She knows the only way to prevent this anxiety is to stop him going out, but he will always go if Josiah calls.

'There's no way out, except by death,' Pa explained once. 'Even those who are too weak or infirm to lift the barrels are called to drive the carts or have goods hidden in their houses.'

Meg bunches her fists, so her nails dig into her palms. If she knew who Josiah was she'd turn him in herself.

Her thoughts are interrupted by a low keening that she doesn't recognise as belonging to any of the estuary creatures. Meg jerks round, her eyes wide, straining to hear more.

Jip scrabbles to his feet, his nails scratching to gain a grip on the slippery wooden floor. Meg can feel tension pulsing from his body and knows he is standing with his head cocked listening too for the sounds from outside.

Meg clutches the window frame. Who is there? And what do they want?

'Please not the excise men,' she mutters to herself in something between a wish and a prayer. 'And please God, Pa is not hurt.'

At that moment she'd barter everything she has and never begrudge another waistcoat for her father to be safe.

She hurries back across the room and gathers her thick woollen shawl around herself to cover her chemise.

She pushes her feet into her wooden pattens and with Jip pressing tightly to her legs she descends the steep wooden stairs as quietly as she can.

2

Meg's heart thumps as the soles of her wooden shoes crunch on the flagstone floor of the Alehouse, despite her efforts to tiptoe. She holds her breath.

As she passes through the bar, she stops to pick up a heavy iron poker from by the fireplace. Although she trusts Jip to protect her, the Alehouse is remote.

Warily, she lifts the metal latch that secures the door to the yard and pulls it open. The old hinges creak like a hangman's gibbet and there is no hiding the fact the door has been opened.

Outside the air is chilly, but the dark of night has given way to monotone grey of dawn. As her eyes adjust, Meg can see the masts of moored boats as silhouettes on the river and hears insects clicking as they start the day. A blackbird flies past, issuing an indignant alarm at the early morning intruders.

Meg shivers as the dawn cold laps her

bare ankles and Jip stands beside her, the fur on his back bristling and a low growl in his throat. She peers out. A couple of figures melt into the shadow of the outbuildings that Pa uses for brewing.

'Who's there?' Meg demands, putting a hand on Jip's head to stop him barking. His presence is reassuring but her heart is still thumping, and her hand weighs the poker.

One of the figures, a large oilskin hiding his real shape, steps forward.

'Meggie, love. You shouldn't be up at this time of day.'

'Pa!' Meg claps a hand to her chest. 'You're making the devil of a noise. Whatever is the matter? Why haven't you come in to bed?'

''Tis young Nat Stowell. We had a run in with the revenue men and he's taken a musket ball in the leg,' her father says. 'We had to hide from them and then carry him along the coast, keeping to the scrub so we weren't seen. It's taken a while.'

Her father's voice has a tremor and is

11

laced with worry and shock.

Meg frowns and picks her way across to the yard to what appears to be a pile of clothing on the ground.

Staring down she realises the bundle is a boy, somewhat younger than herself, his face not yet growing hair and his body not filled out.

'He's but a child.' Meg turns to her father, her tone accusatory. 'What is he doing out on a run?'

Her father shrugs and spreads his hands.

'Short-handed,' he says. 'But Josiah needed to unload and move the barrels inland, so Harry brought along his brother to help as a tubsman.'

Meg thins her lips.

The night business is hard labour and many of the tubsmen who haul the barrels off the boats are bent and crooked from the work. But that is the least of their worries.

Dodging the excise men who patrol the coastline seeking out the smugglers is a constant contest. If they are found unloading a boat at night, the uniformed men hold the upper hand with their muskets and the rule of law on their side.

Tonight, however, it seems the excise men discovered them.

Her father waves a hand towards the figure still lurking in the shadow of the Brewhouse, a wide-brimmed hat pulled low over his eyes.

Meg crouches down beside the boy. His breathing is raspy, his face a pale moon with a sheen across his forehead. She glances back up at her father and clicks her tongue.

'Best get the boy inside,' she says. 'I can do nothing out here in the yard. Though I don't know I'll do any better indoors.'

Her father gives a nod and beckons another figure loitering in the shadow. Together they pick up the boy, Pa taking his feet and the man Meg presumes is Harry, his shoulders. Nat gives a low moan and Meg glances round, conscious of how sound carries at night.

'Take him up to my room,' Meg says as

her father gives her a questioning look.

Between them, the men manhandled the boy into the pub and up the steep stairs to Meg's room. Harry goes first, backwards, halting on each tread so that Pa can catch up. Meg catches sight of the boy's face, crumpled in pain. He twists in their grasp and stiffens, biting down on his lip until it bleeds.

Jip follows, sniffing at the strangers.

Meg pushes the outer door shut and puts the wooden bar across it. She returns the poker to the fireplace, lights a taper from the glowing embers of the fire in the bar, and shields it as she climbs the stairs after the men. Jip follows her, his tail wagging, easily pleased with the early morning excitement.

Pa and Harry set Nat down on Meg's pallet and Pa stands back while Harry brushes the hair from his brother's face and whispers to him.

'So, the excise men were after you?' Meg asks, looking from one to the other.

Besides the excise men, there are other gangs of smugglers along the coast who would happily muscle in on trade if anything were to happen to Josiah's gang, and fights between the smugglers are more common than the run-ins with the law.

'Aye,' Pa says, shuffling from foot to foot and looking contrite.

'Then the chances are they'll call here, looking for contraband. You know William Rufus has it in for you. You haven't put any in the outhouses, have you?' Meg's voice is fierce. They need no further excuses for that man to come sniffing round the Alehouse.

Pa shakes his head.

'No, it's all been moved inland,' he whispers. 'Disappeared into the landscape. They won't find it. We were unlucky, just finishing up when they caught us.'

Meg looks down at Nat. His eyelids flicker, and he is ashen and perspiring while his short dark hair is matted and clumped to his head. His breath is ragged, and all his clothing is damp. His moaning has subsided, which is worrying.

'We'd best get him out of these wet clothes and then put him in the attic where the revenue is less likely to look,' she says. 'I'll fetch a dry shirt if the two of you will strip him.'

She goes to her father's room and takes a clean but old linen shirt from his chest and hands it to the men.

They change Nat's clothing and heave a spare straw pallet up the ladder into the attic.

Harry then climbs up and Pa lifts the boy to him. Nat is not big, but the manoeuvre is tricky, and he hisses with pain, as he is jolted about.

Jip whines in sympathy and circles the base of the ladder, knowing he can't get up there.

Meg lights a candle stump with the taper, kicks off her pattens and climbs up the ladder into the attic, taking the boy's clothing with her. She hangs his breeches, stockings, and shirt from the ends of the rafters and sends Harry down to collect his jacket and boots.

'Make sure there's no sign of him,' she

tells Harry.

Meanwhile she sets the candle down beside Nat and looks at his leg. The boy's face in the flickering candlelight shines like a polished table.

She sends Pa to fetch a rag and water. Harry drops his brother's clothing in a corner and comes to crouch beside her. He has removed his hat and his blond hair flops over his face. A sharp smell of wood smoke and fish rises from him, and Meg notes the crease of worry across his face.

Harry straightens Nat's legs and glances up at Meg. A long, ragged tear appears in the fleshy calf of his right leg. The skin around it is bloodied, discoloured, and pulverized. Nat winces as Meg pokes it with a finger, and mutters but his eyes remain shut.

'Happen I can try and get it out with a knife,' Meg says glancing up at Harry. He grimaces. He is cradling his brother's head in his hands.

She doesn't need to spell out the danger the boy is in and how likely it is the wound will kill him.

Harry nods.

'I'd take him to the surgeon,' he whispers. 'But the excise men are out searching, and I'd have to ask Amos to borrow his cart.'

They both look down at Nat. Meg doesn't say it, but they both know a twenty-mile journey to Kirkstainton, rattling over muddy rutted roads, wouldn't do the boy any good, either. He is as well off taking his chances here.

Pa will have some brandy they can give him for the pain and tomorrow she can go to Mistress Cooper and get something for fever and for healing or, if Harry chooses, he can go to town and fetch some laudanum.

But before Meg can go downstairs for a knife there is a thumping on the front door and below them Jip begins barking frantically and jumping around.

'The excise men!' Harry hisses.

Meg glances up and sees fear etched into his face. Several things flash through her mind at the same time.

They can't move the boy.

Harry can't be found here.

And everything must appear to be normal.

There is a knocking in her chest as her heart beats faster and a spike of adrenaline surges round her body. She squeezes her fists closed and makes a decision.

3

'I'll go.' Meg hisses at Harry. 'Stay here. Pull the ladder up behind me and shut the trap door. 'And,' she glances at Nat. 'Keep him quiet, however you can. Pa, go to bed, now!'

Meg lets her father descend first and then hurries down the ladder. She is aware of Harry pulling it back up and closing the trap as she puts on her pattens and deliberately thumps down the staircase.

The Alehouse, little more than a converted cottage with the bar downstairs and two small bedrooms above and a small outhouse behind that Meg uses as a kitchen, is chilly.

The air is always damp, especially in winter when the sea fret eddies around, or wind and rain blow in from the open ocean threatening to wash them all away.

Once, when she was younger and her mother was still alive, the sea advanced over the dyke and cloudy waters swirled and lapped at the door to the Alehouse.

Meg had come down in the morning to find Pa lifting the stools on to the tables and her mother moving cooking pots and pushing baskets of onions and potatoes on to shelves out of reach of the flood.

When the water receded a muddy residue was left that took days to sweep away. For a long time, it seemed everything they touched or ate had a gritty taste. Meg lives in fear of the sea rising again but so far, the dyke has held, and the sea has stayed where it is supposed to be.

The hammering becomes even more intense, shaking the door in its frame as Meg struggles to lift the wooden bar.

She has to grab hold tight of Jip as his hackles are up and a deep rolling growl comes from within him. He would love to take a chunk out of the men who crowd into the doorway, pushing the door so it flies open narrowly missing hitting Meg in the face.

William Rufus steps into the Alehouse,

his two aides almost falling in behind him. Both have a musket slung over their shoulders and are panting with the effort of banging on the door.

'Where is it?' William demands. 'I know your father was out this night.'

William's face is flushed, he has streaks of mud over his britches and boots and his red tunic is somewhat awry. Meg takes a small sliver of comfort that the excise men have had as busy a night as the smugglers.

'Father is in his bed,' she says primly. 'As was I until this last minute when someone rudely banged on the door.'

'We're searching the premises,' William says, glaring at her.

'Fine,' Meg replies, pulling her shawl closer as the draft from the door swirls around her thin chemise. She goes to the grate in the public room and tosses more logs on the fire.

The flag-stoned floor is cold and the sawdust she throws down to keep the Alehouse smelling fresh blows into the corners with the breeze from the door.

She hears William and his men clatter upstairs and her father's protests as they yank him from his bed. She guesses they treat him none too gently and she finds a wry pleasure in this. It is, after all, his own fault. If he wasn't involved in the night business there would be no reason for the excise men to be here at all.

The footsteps move overhead into her room and the floorboards creak in protest. Meg hears the shutters pushed back further with a familiar screech of sound. She hopes the men haven't treated them ill. The wood is only held together with cobwebs as it is.

She thinks of her petticoat hung from a nail in the wall, her blanket tossed aside as they laid Nat on her pallet, her linen box and her cape and bonnet behind the door. Not much for them to search and certainly nowhere to hide anchors of brandy, kegs of Holland's gin or packages of lace and fine cloth.

William leads the way back downstairs, his men following like anxious puppies. Meg stands with her arms folded across her chest watching them.

'Brewhouse?' William holds out his hand.

Meg hands over the large, wrought-iron key, knowing the excise men will find only barrels of her father's homemade ale and an anchor of brandy stamped duty paid. The further outhouses are for overwintering the goat and a wood store. There are no hiding places here.

The goods they are looking for will have been salted away inland and carefully concealed.

'Pah,' William almost spits at her as he returns and flings the key back. Meg fingers the familiar ironwork, the shape of the bow reminding her of the leading in the church windows.

'We'll catch him at it one day. We'll rid this coast of smugglers. You see if we don't.'

The two aides leave first and as Meg stands beside the back door ready to shut it behind them, William stops and turns to her.

'You don't have to live like this, Meg

Parton. There's a fine stone house in town waiting if you'll only say yes.'

William's voice is oily and the sound of it makes Meg itch. She steps back, but William is no respecter of space and moves closer. His breath carries the stink of rotting meat.

'I'll have your father sometime, Meg. Then you'll have no option but to take me up on my offer. You'll not get a better one.' He stands taller and straightens his hat. 'Don't think you will.'

Meg feels his eyes run up and down over her. She notices he starts as he looks at her chemise. She glances down and sees a smear of blood, no longer the crimson of ripe apples but a burnt umber iron colour.

She feels a flush spread across her face and is clutching for an excuse when William sneers, the scar at the edge of his lip pulling down his mouth on one side.

He was wounded fighting the Frenchies and Meg has no doubt he is a brave man, doing his best as he sees it for King and country. But she has no wish to marry him, not even for a proper house in town, built of even stones, with glass windows, a fine drawing-room, and a maid to cook and clean.

She blinks and swallows. It's not true. She'd love it all — except William. Perhaps she is a fool. Any other girl would be overjoyed to be married and living in luxury, but there is a coldness to William that she cannot fathom, and he loves his work too much.

The people who live around the estuary have barely enough to live on and earning a little extra from the night business is what keeps most of them alive.

Besides which, the duty of imported goods has priced things like tea and sugar beyond the means of many.

Meg knows that further along the coast the excise men take a cut of the smuggling that goes on under their noses and allow the trade to go ahead. Not William, though. It seems to be his life's work to do whatever it takes to enforce the law.

Not for the first time she wonders if William's wish to marry her is less to do with herself and more to do with stopping her father working for Josiah.

Meg shakes her head and watches as William steps outside and clicks his fingers. One of his aides scurries over, pulling his horse. The beast is reluctant, stiffens its legs and shows the whites of its eyes. William is oblivious and mounts.

She pushes the door shut before William can turn and look at her again and puts the heavy bar back in place. She swallows the bile that has risen in her throat and finds herself shaking. She leans against the door and allows herself to slide to the floor.

There are times, like now, when Meg misses her mother and longs for comfort and advice. What would her mother think of William? Would she advocate for the marriage?

Meg remembers the way her Pa looked at Ma. Her mother had been a beauty, with long auburn hair, blue eyes, and lovely skin. She had left her family, running away to marry Pa, and they had settled at the cottage on the estuary when Pa gave up working on the boats.

He'd learned the business of brewing and opened the Alehouse, many of their customers visiting especially to be served by Ma. She was a favourite of everyone, and Pa was devastated by her death from a fever she caught during one damp river winter.

A lump rises in Meg's throat as she thinks of her mother, but with the thought comes the realisation that William doesn't look at her with that same adoration. The spark that Ma and Pa had is missing.

Jip nudges her with his head. He sees it as a game when she sits on the floor. Absentmindedly she strokes him, and he flops down, half in her lap and half on the flagstones.

'Oh, Jip. What am I going to do?' she says.

There is no way she wants to be hand-fasted to William Rufus, yet if Pa is caught smuggling and sentenced to hang, what choice would she have?

'It is not fair, Jip,' she whispers as a

large tear rolls down her cheek. Jip licks her hand. 'If only he would leave off the night business, I wouldn't have to worry.'

4

Meg listens as the sound of the horses' hooves fades away. The excise men's visit has taken less than fifteen minutes, but she is now wide awake, and it is light outside.

Aware that there is a full day's work ahead, plus Nat in the attic, Meg dries her eyes with the edge of her shawl and scrambles to her feet.

Spidery fingers of daylight appear round the shutters of the tiny kitchen. Meg pushes open the wooden panels and looks out on to the grasslands behind the dyke, where low mist hovers eerily just above the ground and the sky is painted with red and orange streaks.

She can hear the wading birds on the estuary squabbling over the best feeding spots.

Oyster catchers fly over the mist with their black and white plumage and bright red legs and beaks, whistling at each other as they swing into land, disappearing into the swirling white vapour.

Closer to the Alehouse, between the sedges and grasses, a white egret picks its way carefully about on its long legs like the stilt walkers that Meg had seen at the summer fair one year.

Meg chides herself for worrying about her own problems when that poor boy is lying upstairs with a musket ball buried in his flesh. She searches around the kitchen for a sharp knife, one with a good point, and a wooden spoon.

She climbs the stairs and calls softly for Harry to lower the ladder. Her legs and feet are so chilled from the stone floors she finds it difficult to scramble up the rungs and when she eventually pulls herself into the attic, she finds Harry sitting beside his brother, Nat's head in his hands.

Meg puts the knife down beside them. Nat's face is pale, and his breathing is shallow.

'Do you think brandy might help?' Meg asks. 'There's some in the Brewhouse.'

Harry looks up and nods.

As daylight spills in through the thin thatch like stars twinkling in the night sky, the attic is lighter. It is the first time Meg has seen Harry's face and it is drawn with worry, his eyes deep sunk.

His face and hands are the colour of imported mahogany wood and Meg guesses he works either on the boats or as a labourer in the fields. His cheek-bones are pronounced and the shadow of a beard dusts his chin.

Meg stands and climbs back down the ladder. Jip is waiting for her and follows her as she goes out to the Brewhouse. She can see the work of William's men. Barrels have been moved about and the sacks of grain sliced open, the contents spilling on the ground.

She clicks her tongue. Pa will have his work cut out today.

She draws a tankard of brandy from the barrel and returns to the attic. Harry lifts Nat's head as Meg holds the tankard to his lips.

'Take a drink, Nat,' Harry urges,

stroking his brother's forehead.

Meg tips the mug and liquid spills down Nat's chin but Meg is pleased to see he wrinkles his nose and flinches, then makes a choking sound as at least some of the fiery liquid goes down his throat. When Harry tries to give him more, Nat jerks away. Meg takes this as a good sign, but Nat is barely sensible.

Harry holds out his hand and Meg passes him the tankard. She arches an eyebrow as he takes a swig of the liquid, wipes his mouth with the back of a hand before putting the brandy down and picking up the knife.

Meg glances across at him a quizzical expression on her face. She doesn't know Harry or Nat. They are not local but then she has barely been more than five miles from the Alehouse in all her life. Still, if Pa trusts them, and trusts them enough to bring them to The Anchor, she will, too.

Harry lowers the knife again to shrug his jacket off and she sees he is broad-shouldered. He wears a thick, cream shirt that is marked and stained, not least with some of Nat's blood, and a leather jerkin over it. His breeches are well worn and muddy and his leather boots are scuffed and marked.

Even with daylight spitting through the thin areas of thatch, the light is not good in the attic, but in the glow of the candle stub, Meg notices Harry's grey eyes, his most startling feature, the same colour as the sky on a stormy strung-out day.

Nat has grey eyes, too, but they are flecked with brown, and flicker between open and closed.

'You're sure?' Meg checks, nodding towards the knife.

She sees Harry swallow and barely incline his head.

'Better if it's me,' he murmurs, so Meg moves and takes up position by Nat's head.

She edges the handle of the wooden spoon between his teeth, so he has something to bite down on, then she holds tight to one of his hands.

She passes Harry the water and rag her father brought up earlier and Harry does his best to clean the wound, but Nat's calf is a mess and it's hard to see where the musket ball lies.

Harry runs his hands over Nat's flesh, feeling out the lead sphere.

Meg does her best to comfort Nat as he writhes and twists in pain. She holds his shoulders as firmly as she can as Harry digs in.

Nat grunts and splutters and from the floor below, Jip howls in sympathy. Harry takes a deep breath, wipes a hand across his brow and continues.

There is a great deal of blood but eventually, he lifts the ball triumphantly between his forefinger and thumb. Nat is dry sobbing; Pa's shirt is damp with sweat and the air in the attic feels thick and close. Harry slips the musket ball into his pocket and Meg offers him a rag to staunch the bleeding.

'Wash it with brandy,' she advises. 'I'll go to Mistress Cooper when I'm in the village and see if she has something for healing. Meanwhile I can get some bread from downstairs to draw any bad humours.'

Harry nods. The corners of his mouth are pulled down as he looks at his brother.

'I'll go and fetch the bread and stoke up the fires and put some gruel on,' Meg says. She glances from one brother to the other.

Nat is darker and his hair shorter, badly hacked in clumps and she wonders if he did it himself. Harry's hair is blonder and flops across his forehead, but they have similar sharp cheeks and grey eyes and there is no missing the connection between them.

She climbs down the ladder again and slips into her room to dress, remembering she has been sitting in her chemise for the last hour and it is further streaked with Nat's blood.

The excise men have pulled her smalls out of her linen chest and her face flushes with the thought. She pulls a face as she laces her boots and goes down the stairs to light the fires properly and start some breakfast for them.

For a moment she stands staring into the flames as they leap about to take hold of the logs. She is still cold and although the fire is bright it is not yet warming the room.

She starts as her father comes down the stairs behind her.

'How is he?' Pa asks.

'We got the ball out,' Meg says, spreading her hands. 'But . . . you know.'

Pa nods. They all know the danger of infection and how easily a life can be snuffed out.

'I'll go to the Mistress Cooper later,' Meg adds. 'Meanwhile, let me take yesterday's bread up to Harry for the wound and I'll sort out some breakfast.'

Pa looks at her.

'You're a good girl, Meggie,' he says.

Meg snorts.

'Happen if you weren't out at night this wouldn't happen,' she says more sharply than she intends. 'And William's men searched the Brewhouse,' she adds. 'They've split the sacks. There's a heap of clearing up to do.'

Pa nods slowly.

'I'll go and sort it,' he says. 'They knew there would be nothing to find here. It was just mean-spirited of them to come, venting their anger.'

Meg rolls her eyes. They could all do without the extra work. Doesn't Pa see that?

As he opens the back door and goes out, Meg puts a pan of water on the grate to boil and throws in oats. She finds yesterday's bread and climbs back up the stairs and then the ladder.

Morning has hardly begun but she feels as if she has done a day's work already. She is not sure how she'll get through until this evening.

She hands Harry the nub of bread.

'Bind it tight around the wound,' she tells him.

Harry nods.

'Thank you,' he says, looking up and fixing his grey eyes on her. The look seems to drill into her as if he can read her deepest secrets and she can't help shivering. 'For helping.'

'I'll fetch some breakfast,' she says, looking away. 'I'll need to milk the goat first, though.'

Meg turns as calmly as she can manage and climbs down the ladder to begin what she fears will be a long day.

Inside her though, her heart flutters in her chest as if a moth has been caught against the window glass. It's an odd feeling that she's never noticed before, but not entirely unpleasant.

5

Meg carries out her early morning chores acutely aware of Nat and Harry upstairs, hidden away. She milks the goat and tethers her out on the grassland.

The morning air, as the early mist rises, is fresh and crisp with a tang of salt, and it is hard to believe out here what has been happening inside.

A skein of geese flies overhead, honking at each other to help them stay in formation. Meg lets the chickens out of the coop and collects the eggs.

She will take some to Mistress Cooper and exchange them for a salve. Something to bring down the fever she can see on Nat's brow. As she works, Jip sniffs around, moving with his long loping stride, no doubt smelling the fox from the previous night.

Back inside, as Meg waits for the gruel to heat, she sweeps out the public room and lays fresh sawdust. The work is at last beginning to warm her through. When the breakfast is ready, she puts a spoonful of tea in the pot and calls her father in from the Brewhouse.

She dishes out bowls of gruel and adds a pinch of salt, fresh milk, and a spoonful of honey to each. She pushes the bowl across the table to her father and pours him some tea.

'I'll take this upstairs,' she says, picking up another bowl.

Jip follows her to the bottom of the ladder.

'Harry!' she calls softly.

His head appears through the attic hatch.

'Breakfast,' she says.

Harry shakes his head.

Meg clicks her tongue.

'Please,' she says, forcing a smile on her face. 'See if Nat will take some and if not, you eat it. It won't do for both of you to be ill. We'll have to open the Alehouse as usual or it will look odd, though I doubt the excise men will be back today.

'You'll have to stay up here, out of the way. I'm away to the village to see Mistress Cooper but Pa will be downstairs if you need anything.'

Harry is persuaded to come down the ladder and take the bowl of gruel and a beaker of fresh milk.

'Thank you,' he mutters without meeting her eye.

He doesn't appear grateful, and Meg has to bite her tongue so she doesn't bid him leave if he wishes.

But as soon as she's thought it, she regrets it. There is no way that Nat can be moved at the moment. Pa has brought them here and now none of them has a choice.

By the time she has parcelled up the eggs in some straw and put them in her wicker basket, wrapped her shawl around herself and listened to Pa grumbling about the damage the excise men have caused, Meg is pleased to escape the Alehouse.

She walks towards the village with a spring in her step. It is good to be outside.

Jip scampers beside her, rushing off to sniff at clumps of grass or investigate piles of seaweed on the muddy riverbank brought in on the tide.

The breeze is pleasant after being in the stuffy attic. Whenever Nat is well enough, she thinks, they should move him downstairs. It would be cooler for him.

As she passes the staithes, two cutters are lined up, unloading goods on to the wooden quay. Men totter up the single planks from the boats on to the dock, carrying towering bundles of goods.

Wood, coal, and grain are unloaded here, while wool and cloth are loaded up for the return journeys. From the other boat, a man is throwing sacks to the men on the wharf who pile them up, ready to reload the smaller boats or wagons that wait nearby.

A warehouse behind the dyke has its main doors open and a watchman is lolling on a stool in the entrance. He takes his clay pipe from his mouth and bids Meg a good morning.

Behind the warehouse is the rope-walk, and men are twisting the twine, working it into long lengths for rigging and mooring lines. Several of them have a rasping cough from the hemp dust in the air that gets into their lungs.

The other side of the ropewalk is the smithy where Owen and Francis, two brothers, work together making and repairing the iron work for the ships. The smithy clangs with sound and even from a distance Meg can feel the heat from the fire.

She loves that smell of hot metal and on the days when she has time, she stops to watch them bend and twist the iron into shape. Nails, hooks, rowlocks — these men can make things up to the size of an anchor for a big ship.

Back at the staithes, the longshoremen nod a greeting to Meg. She recognises many of them. They come into the Ale-house when their shift is finished. One straightens up, rubs his back, and pushes his hat further back on his head.

'Morning, Miss Meg,' he calls.

'Good morning, Arthur,' Meg calls back.

'How is your Pa?' the man asks.

Meg shrugs.

'He's well, thank you kindly,' she says.

Arthur nods his head slowly.

'Good, good,' he says, holding his hat in place as he speaks.

Another man comes up behind Arthur and claps him on the back and the two move off to something else, leaving Meg to continue on her way.

She thinks back over the conversation and frowns.

Why should Arthur be asking particularly after Pa? The chances are that he'll be in the Alehouse in a few hours. Unless, perhaps, Arthur is aware of last night's business?

A cart rattles past her, pulled by a single plodding horse that snorts fusty warm breath, and Meg has to step off the dyke to give it room to pass. The driver tips his hat in acknowledgement as he goes by.

The day feels completely normal, but

Meg is wound up taught and flooded with adrenaline. She sees everything in extra colour and tuned to different sounds and smells.

She carries on walking until she reaches the village, little more than a collection of low thatched houses around a covered stone marketplace, where farmers bring their goods every week to sell. The distinctive smell of wood smoke from the chimneys scents the air.

Further inland, on a slight rise behind the village, is the parish church, built in the ruins of a monastery destroyed by the King a couple of hundred years previously.

Most of the stone was spirited away by locals for their own building projects, but around the church it is possible to see low walls and foundations of a once great religious place.

One family who took the stones were the ancestors of the squire who lives in a grand house outside the village. Most of the people who live in the village are employed on the estate in some way.

The squire owns or part owns many of the ships that pull in at the staithes, too. Pa is one of the few people who is not beholden to Squire Padgett.

Several women stand outside the village shop, baskets over their arms, chattering away. They pause as Meg approaches and Meg feels the colour rise in her face.

'Morning,' she greets them and dips her head.

'Good morning, Meg,' they chorus but Meg wonders how genuine they are. The world has tilted, and she can't tell up from down or normal from unusual.

Often, she would stop and pass a few words with them but this morning she steps inside on to the hard earthen floor. Inside the ceiling is low and it is dim with dust motes dancing in the dull light from the small windows.

The shop is the downstairs room of a normal cottage with a big fireplace on one side and sacks of dry goods piled across the floor and a rough counter with stone jars and baskets on it.

'Morning, Meg,' Mr Bracken says, rubbing a hand down his rough sacking apron. 'What can I get you?'

'Just some flour,' Meg says. She was planning on making pies today, but she doesn't feel up to it now. Instead, she'll add dumplings to the stew pot to fill the men up. There are some herbs in the garden she can add for flavour. 'Oh, and butter, too, please.'

She watches Mr Bracken weigh out her order and wrap the items in brown paper. Then she hands over her coins and hurries out.

The women are still outside and again pausing their chatter as she leaves. She can feel their gaze on her back, stabbing like a hundred bee stings as she walks away.

She carries on along the street to the last of the cottages, at a slight distance from its neighbours, a run-down single storey with a tiny lean-to shed on the side and an overgrown garden that almost hides it from the road.

She is about to approach when she

hears the hollow step of a horse coming towards her. She glances up and is appalled to see William Rufus on horseback accompanied by his two lackeys who run to keep up with him.

William is somewhat better turned out now, Meg notices. His breeches have been cleaned and his hair is tidy under his hat. He must have been home to change after searching The Anchor.

He does not look in a better mood however, and although he calls out brightly enough, 'Good morning, Miss Parton,' Meg hears an undertone of malevolence in his voice that makes her stomach squirm.

6

Meg turns and pastes a smile on her face. 'Mister Rufus,' she says. 'We meet again.'

'It's Sergeant,' William says crisply. 'And I'm looking for someone who is injured and might be after something for a wound,' he pauses. 'From someone like Mistress Cooper. Now why would you be visiting this witch?'

Meg flinches and feels rather than hears a rumble in the back of Jip's throat.

Those who don't know her often called Mistress Cooper a witch. Indeed, Meg and her friends had done so when they were small and knew no better, but Mistress Cooper, Meg now realises, is only about the same age as her father.

Her very pale skin, white hair, and pinkish eyes single her out as unusual and coupled with her love of plants and herbs and knowledge of cures makes her different enough from the other villagers to be avoided unless her help is needed.

Mistress Cooper keeps herself to herself; no doubt aware that anyone can turn on her at any moment and blame her for any bad luck they have suffered.

Meg thinks quickly. She didn't like lying but William will need something to satisfy his curiosity. If not, he is likely to follow her inside to Mistress Cooper's cottage.

'Burns,' she says, pulling her free hand from her apron pocket along with her handkerchief and deftly using her thumb to keep it in place around her other fingers.

'I burned myself on the pan this morning making gruel. If I'm to cook this evening I must have something to ease the pain.

William's eyes narrow as he looks at her.

Meg wonders if he will demand to inspect the wound but at that moment, she hears the cottage door swing open and turns to see Mistress Cooper framed in the doorway.

Meg gives William a brief smile and hurries towards her, Jip hugging her skirts.

'Mistress Cooper!' Meg is aware she is gushing.

The pale woman's pink eyes peer at her and then a smile of recognition crosses her face.

'Meg Parton, good morning. Come in.'

Mistress Cooper stands back and allows Meg and Jip access. As Meg turns to address her, she is aware Mistress Cooper is still looking out into the road and further that William Rufus is still there on his horse, watching.

For a moment she feels she is in the middle of a stand-off between William and Mistress Cooper but as soon as the door closes behind her, a sense of relief washes over her. She only wishes the closing of a door could solve more problems.

Inside the cottage blacken beams run across the ceiling with bunches of drying plants hanging all along them.

The walls are lined with wooden shelving, which holds baskets, jars, and bowls of more vegetation — seed heads, nuts, pieces of bark. A good fire burns the fireplace, puffing a little smoke back into the cottage.

Most of the room is taken up by an oversized table that is covered with stone jars, clay pots, several pestles and mortars, small bottles and papers with tiny coppery script and diagrams drawn on them. The floor is covered in straw and several small barrels are lined up along one wall.

Mistress Cooper looks like night and day. Her skin is pale and white, but she wears a dark dress with the sleeves pushed up above the elbows. A whitish mob cap, garnished with twigs and leaves, surrounds her face while a well-stained apron provides the only colour — splotches of green, red, pinks and orange cover the fabric, as if a rainbow has fallen from the sky and melted on it.

'I was expecting you,' Mistress Cooper says. 'Something for fever, healing and pain, I'll warrant.' She moves towards the table and begins rustling around amongst the things on it.

Meg's eyes open wider.

'How?' she gasps. If the woman had said she'd come for something for a burn she wouldn't have been surprised. She might have overheard the conversation outside with William Rufus, but fever? Pain? Healing? How does she glean this from Meg's arrival?

'The gift of second sight!' The old woman smiles at Meg's surprise and taps her nose with a long finger.

Mistress Cooper spins fortunes at the quarter fairs and she has a knack for knowing what was going on in the village without appearing to move from her house.

Those who whisper about witchcraft and trickery hush when they need her cures and help as there is no doctor nearby and it is twenty miles to Kirkstainton. They turn a blind eye as she collects herbs and berries from the hedgerows and wanders around at night, a basket over her arm, muttering to herself.

'Yes,' Meg stutters. Could Mistress Cooper have heard about the night business and know of Nat and Harry? 'And something for bleeding, too.'

'Best make a poultice of bread and yeast for that,' Mistress Cooper says. 'Willow bark for fever. You'll need that, no doubt, and a salve of comfrey and anemone for the healing.'

She rummages around, picking from the dried vegetation and concoctions from bottles on the shelves. She pulls each thing close to her face looking at it from just a few inches away before deciding if it is what she needs or not.

When she has collected the ingredients in one place, she pulls off the heads of the plants and spills in a few drops of a solution, working the mixture together with a pestle and mortar as Meg watches.

Jip, relaxed in the cottage, slopes off towards the fire and lies down on the reed mat in front of it. Very soon the sounds of his snores join the chopping and grinding sounds from Mistress Cooper.

'Make a tea from this.' Mistress Cooper presses a bundle into Meg's hands. It feels like lumps of wood. 'A couple of pieces boiled up in water. You can add a drop of honey if you must. This is important. The most important. The tea will act on the fever and bring down swelling,' she emphasises.

She returns to the table and works something else before handing Meg a small earthenware bowl of paste.

'Apply to the wound,' she says. 'And take care of your father.'

Meg frowns and stares at her. Pa? Why? He's not sick, but Mistress Cooper makes no effort to explain.

Meg chooses not to argue. She doesn't want to explain it is not Pa who is ill, and they have someone else in the Alehouse.

That would involve talking about the gunshot and then what they were all doing out that night and word might get back to the excise men. She doesn't need them snooping round again.

She swallows. She doesn't need William Rufus snooping round at all. He is becoming more persistent in his pursuit of her, and it seems more persistent in closing in on Josiah's smuggling operation.

She wishes he'd move further up the coast and concentrate on Jack Savage's gang. The word is they move goods almost every night. By comparison, Josiah's is a small operation, barely worthy of William's attention, but it's somehow stuck in his craw and he won't let it go.

She looks up to see Mistress Cooper watching her closely.

'Should I get some laudanum?' she asks.

Mistress Cooper scowls.

'Only if you want vivid dreams and wandering nightmares,' she scoffs. 'This,' she waves a hand at the paste and bottle she'd given Meg, 'will do him well if applied properly.'

Meg is cheered by this. She'll tell Harry. It's better if there is no need to journey all the way to Kirkstainton.

'Thank you,' she whispers. 'For all the advice.'

Mistress Cooper thins her lips before speaking.

'Best thing is to sort it all out, once and for all,' she says.

Again, Meg is confused by what the woman says. It seems as if she is saying one thing but taking part in another conversation all together. She gives a quick nod and leaves the eggs on the table before putting the willow bark and salve in her basket with the flour and butter.

'Come, Jip,' she says. He follows her to the door and is by her side as she peers each way up and down the street to make sure William Rufus is gone.

Only when she is part way back along the dyke, watching the men rowing boats of goods towards the village, does she think about what Mistress Cooper said as she was leaving.

Sort what out? Did she mean the smuggling? Or William's advances?

And how is Meg to sort out either situation? Her father has made clear that the night business is men's business. He won't have her interfering and besides, she has no idea who Josiah is.

Pa will support her in whatever she decides about William but if Pa is caught smuggling, what can she do then? Could she keep the Alehouse going on her own?

She doesn't know.

Meg begins the walk home with her head down, deep in thought.

7

Meg has passed the staithes and the warehouses and is almost home when she hears the voice behind her and hears an uneven footstep. She stops and turns, a smile cracking across her face like a wave breaking on the shoreline.

Jip gives a yip of delight and bounds back to the person following them, dancing round her as she bends to pat him.

'Eliza!' Meg says. 'I didn't see you.'

'I've been following you since the village, but you didn't hear me calling,' Eliza said. 'You were deep in thought, perhaps?'

Meg gives a quick smile.

'I need to get back and get some food on,' she blusters. 'It's been a busy morning.'

She has known Eliza since they were in the church school together. Meg had excelled at learning her letters, but Eliza had been better at needlework.

Together they had helped each other stumble through a morning's lessons and avoid the cane the mistress was inclined to use if their work was not up to standard. Pa had said they were lucky to be getting an education, but Meg hadn't always agreed with him.

Her friend has thick, dark, curly hair that is barely contained by her bonnet. As a child Meg had run her hands through Eliza's hair, marvelling at the way it bounced back into position after being straightened.

For a long time, she wished for hair like it and more than once her Ma had rocked her to sleep as she moaned about her own dirty yellow, straight locks.

Contrasting with her dark hair Eliza has pale skin, and her cheeks have two small red blooms from the effort of walking fast. She wears a fashionable dress with a high waist and puffed sleeves, and rather than a thick shawl she wears a short jacket over it.

Eliza is beautiful and Meg has always admired the way she is delightfully turned out despite living in no better circumstances than Meg does.

Eliza's father, a soldier, was killed when she was small, fighting the French, and her mother, a dressmaker, was left with a small child. Besides the needlework, she takes in washing and does repairs to keep a roof over their heads.

Eliza is also a needlewoman, but she was born with a withered arm and severe limp. Meg barely notices this as Eliza copes so well, but her deformities have undoubtedly affected her marriage prospects.

Eliza now rubs her bad leg with her good hand as Jip nudges her arm for more cuddles.

Eliza giggles and bends down to pet him.

'Enough, Jip. You know I love you,' she says, and Meg's dog spins round after his tail in a frenzy of showing off.

'Sometimes,' Meg says, swinging her basket to her other arm so she can link arms with her friend. 'I think that dog prefers you to me.'

'Nonsense,' Eliza says. 'He would lay down his life for you.'

'On a good day,' Meg says. 'Now were you coming to visit us?'

'I saw you talking to William Rufus in the village,' Eliza says, drawing back from Meg a little.

Meg snorts.

'He was being threatening and bombastic again,' she says. 'His usual self.'

'Has he asked you to marry him again?' Eliza asks, her pale blue eyes on Meg.

For a moment Meg is torn. She knows Eliza longs to be betrothed and to have some security for herself and her mother and she feels guilty that William has settled on herself when her friend is more deserving, but on the other hand William is a driven man and she feels he might be cruel.

She wouldn't wish him on anyone, and she worries that Eliza might overlook this side of him in her desperation to wed.

She swallows.

'He might have mentioned it,' she

says. 'In a roundabout sort of fashion.'

Eliza sighs.

'You know he has a town house,' she says. 'And he has money.'

'A big house isn't everything,' Meg says more snappily than she means to. 'I don't want to marry William Rufus. Not now. Not ever.'

Eliza twirls a strand of her dark hair that has escaped her bonnet, round her finger.

Meg glances at her friend.

'No . . .' She draws the word out. 'Really, Eliza? Are you sure?'

'Well, I don't have many options,' Eliza pouts and waves her bad arm. 'This is the first thing that everyone notices. They can't see past it.'

'That's not true!'

She grew up without a mother and Eliza grew up without a father. For a while she fanatisised about the two families merging but Eliza's mother obviously didn't fancy a life in the Alehouse. She is more genteel than Pa and Meg has long abandoned any hope of bringing them together, but Eliza is still her best friend.

As they stand together, Meg is aware time is spinning past, lapping at her heels like the tide and wheeling by like the arcing seagulls. Eventually she pulls away.

'I have to bake the bread and get a stew made,' she says to Eliza. 'Or there will be men starving tonight. You'll hear their stomach rumbling in the village.'

'Well,' Eliza says, grinning broadly. 'We can't have that. Best get along.'

'Will you come in?' Meg says. 'Walk me home?'

'Certainly,' Eliza agrees.

They set off again, Jip running circles round them until they come to the Alehouse. Meg leads the way into the kitchen and Eliza takes a stool to sit while Meg unpacks her basket.

Meg can hear voices from the bar and knows her father must already have customers. She wonders if there is any word of Harry or Nat.

For a moment she thinks of telling Eliza about them, but she remembers that Eliza has an interest in William Rufus and William has an interest in the smugglers.

'Do you have much work?' she asks Eliza, but barely listens as Eliza describes a dress that her mother is sewing for somebody.

She has noticed Nat's shirt still bundled on the floor in the corner of the kitchen. She mentally kicks herself for being so careless and swiftly scoops it up and places it in a pail.

'Let me just put some water on these,' she says, jerking her head towards the yard and taking the pail out to the pump.

Eliza follows her as Meg pumps water in the pail.

'Pa's,' Meg says with a shrug.

'Really?' Eliza arches an eyebrow.

Meg winces as she realises that Eliza must know all Pa's clothes as she has stitched most of them.

She leaves the pail by the pump and pulls her friend back inside just as Pa comes through from the bar.

'Ah, Meg,' he begins before he sees

Eliza. 'Harry —' He stops abruptly.

'Yes?' Meg asks. Her father got them into this. She wouldn't have to be hiding things from Eliza if there was no smuggling going on.

'Dinner,' her Pa says. 'Was wondering about dinner.'

'Not ready, yet, Pa,' Meg says with a sigh. 'I'm just back from the village. I've the bread and the stew . . .'

She lets the sentence trail away. She's had a busy morning already and there hasn't been time to get a meal ready. Her father should realise this.

Pa fingers his waistcoat, a dark burgundy, which Eliza has stitched with flowers and ivy around the edges and has sewn shell buttons down the front.

'Ah, yes, of course,' he says. 'Of course. I'll tell him. Not to worry. When you're ready.'

He turns tail and goes back into the bar.

Meg is aware of Eliza staring at her and feels the colour rising in her cheeks.

'I swear he gets more and more forgetful as the days go by,' she says with a laugh, but she can tell Eliza is not convinced.

A wave of guilt crests in Meg. She would love to tell Eliza what is going on, but it's too dangerous. Eliza regards her sadly.

'Will I see you at church on Sunday?' she asks.

'Of course,' Meg answers brightly. 'I should have caught up with myself by then.'

'Good,' Eliza says and lifts her good hand.

Jip gets up from the floor and pads to the doorway after her.

'Goodbye, Jip.' Eliza scratches the dog's head.

'Bye, Liza,' Meg calls and waves, as her friend sets off back to the village.

As soon as Eliza is some distance away, Meg grabs the salve she got from Mistress Cooper and hurries up the stairs.

She is shocked to find the ladder is still in place on the first floor. She should have reminded Harry to pull it up and close the hatch; that way they were less likely to be seen if anyone came looking.

It is too late for that now, though. She'll tell him to do it when she leaves.

She climbs the ladder quietly, unsure what she'll find. She half expects Harry to be waiting but when she peers in the attic, she has a momentary glimpse of the brothers asleep, lying side-by-side on the straw pallet, before Harry jumps up, ready to defend Nat.

8

'Only me,' Meg says, leaning back, away from Harry and swaying unsteadily on the ladder.

Harry pauses, relaxes, and steps forward. He takes her hand to stop her falling. His touch burns her skin as if she has lifted a pan without a cloth.

Her heart beats faster and she is very aware of their bodies in the low space of the attic.

'I have some things to help from Mistress Cooper,' she tells Harry. 'Here, apply this salve to the wound and I will make him a tea from willow bark for the fever.'

She hands the salve to Harry and climbs down again.

In the small kitchen she uses the bellows to stir up the fire and fills the large black kettle with water from the pump and hangs it on the hook to heat. While she waits, she sets out onions and the other vegetables she will need for the stew.

When the water is hot, she drops in a couple of pieces of bark in a tankard and adds water, putting the rest of Mistress Cooper's remedy on a shelf out of the way, where neither Jip nor her father are likely to disturb them.

Meg sniffs at the tea. It has a pungent, woody smell. She dips a finger in and tastes it.

Her eyes water and her nose wrinkles. It is bitter. No wonder Mistress Cooper suggested honey. She fetches her pot of honey from the wooden cupboard and spoons in a generous amount.

Before she can take it upstairs, her father comes in from the bar. He looks around carefully before speaking.

'Sorry,' he says. 'I didn't realise Eliza was here. You didn't tell her, did you?'

'No, Pa,' Meg says. 'Although she guessed something is happening. She's not daft. You were behaving most oddly. I told her it was your age.'

Pa wipes a hand over his face and grins.

'Perhaps it is,' he says. 'I'm sorry to put all this on you, Meggie. 'Tis all my fault. Perhaps I shouldn't have brought the lads here.'

'What else were they to do?' Meg says and realises that her father has done what he always does and works a problem round until she agrees with him.

She puts her hands on her hips and scowls at him.

'Don't think I approve of the night business,' she says. 'But 'tis the best thing that you brought Nat here. I don't know where they live but it must be a way to go, and they would never have made it to Kirkstainton.'

Her father nods and rests a hand on her shoulder for a moment.

'I'm grateful to you, Meggie. Just so you know.'

Meg shakes her head as he leaves and scoops up the tankard.

Then she returns to the attic, calling quietly to Harry that she is coming.

She lifts the tankard up to him and he takes it so she can climb the ladder more easily.

The attic has a fetid smell of unwashed bodies and overcrowding. Nat is lying still and silent on the pallet. Meg creeps closer and can feel heat radiating from him. It is like being near a fire. He is burning up.

'We can't move him yet.' Harry brushes his brother's damp hair from his face. 'He's too weak.'

Meg looks at the boy. He appears smaller than ever. His face is pale, almost translucent and his skin is wet with perspiration.

'I'll bring some fresh water up,' Meg says. 'Lay a wet cloth over him and keep it moist. Try to cool him. And the tea.' She indicates the tankard. 'Lift his head and get him to drink. Mistress Cooper was most insistent, and I can make more.'

Harry nods. Meg can see dark shadows under his eyes and is sure, that although he was lying next to Nat, he wasn't sleeping.

'I must go and help my father and put a stew on for this evening's meal.'

Harry nods.

'Of course,' he says. 'We should not have disrupted your lives. We should have tried to make it to Kirkstainton.'

Meg shakes her head.

'You're better here,' she says. 'The travel would not do him well. We'll work it out. But remember, there will be customers below soon. You'll have to stay as quiet as you can.'

She smiles and is rewarded by a slight twitch of Harry's mouth, an attempt at a smile that doesn't reach his eyes. Still, she goes down to the public room with her heart turning somersaults.

She shouldn't be happy they are there. They bring great danger to her father and herself, but she is intrigued by the brothers and wants to get to know them better.

She grins as she cuts the mutton and fills the pot, throwing more scraps to Jip than he deserves.

When she goes out to the garden to collect herbs and greens everything appears brighter, and the birds sing more loudly than usual.

For the next couple days, Nat hangs between life and death and Harry doesn't leave his side. Meg climbs the ladder taking the willow bark tea and fresh water up.

She takes Harry porridge in the mornings, bread and cheese at lunchtimes and whatever is going in the evenings, but often the food remains on his plate when she goes to collect it and Jip has taken to sitting below the ladder waiting to catch the scraps.

Nat's face has lost all tone, and his bones stand out, skull-like. Not only is Nat fading, but Harry is, too. His cheeks are sunken and his eyes, which were so brilliant, have darkened and lost their sparkle. He hunches over his brother as if he would breathe some of his own life into him.

When she has time, Meg sits with them. She hopes her presence gives Harry some comfort and lets him know he is not alone.

'My parents both died of fever,' he

tells her one morning when they can hear Pa singing downstairs. 'There has only been Nat and me for as long as I can remember.

'We've survived with the chickens and the garden. As soon as I could I got a job with a fisherman on the coast, but I don't like to leave Nat for too long. He gets the odd day's labour looking after sheep or harvesting. He's a good lad.'

He looks down at his brother and gives a weak smile.

'When we heard Josiah needed extra men Nat begged me to take him. I blame myself. I should have had better care of him.'

'How long have you been working for Josiah?' Meg asks.

Harry shrugs.

'A year or so. It's good the work is overnight so I'm around in the day for Nat.'

'But it's risking your life every time,' Meg says fiercely. 'And there's always the danger of being caught and hanged.'

'But one night's work pays better

than a week on the fishing boat.' Harry spreads his hands. 'And if the fish aren't running it's more reliable, too.'

Meg presses her lips together.

Living on the coast, she knows about the fishing. Many fish are seasonal and a trip out too early or too late will result in no catch. Still, smuggling shouldn't need to be the answer.

'Were there no batsman to protect you?' Meg asks.

'Aye, one man, but he couldn't watch everywhere. Rufus split his excise men and came at us from two directions. Nat wasn't fast enough to slip away. He isn't used to the coast in the dark.'

He shrugs and gives Meg a long look. Her face warms and her limbs tingle under his gaze. She is glad of the low light in the attic. She wishes they were in a better place to have this conversation — outside walking hand in hand along the riverbank perhaps, rather than whispering over Nat's sick bed.

Meg brings goat's milk up for Nat, which she hopes might strengthen him, and bowls of stew for Harry, but both are left untouched. Nat sleeps for long periods while Harry applies the salve that Mistress Cooper made to his leg and keeps his brother cool with damp cloths.

As the days pass Meg puts off going to the attic — she'll pick some beets from the garden first, or wash out smalls, or boil water for tea.

It will give Nat more time to heal, she tells herself, but all the while she's anxious, holding her breath as she enters the attic, waiting for the tell-tale smell of decay.

For Pa, she puts on a smile, pretending all is well, but as she prepares meals for the Alehouse, she wonders what will happen if Nat doesn't make it. She finds herself making promises she can't keep — she'll be a better person, she'll put an end to Josiah's night business, she'll marry William and settle down.

No!

Meg swallows. She can't make promises like that.

So, she approaches the attic with a

dry mouth and tight throat, fearing the worst, but although Nat's injury is open, angry and red, it does not blacken, and it seems that Nat may yet survive.

9

During the day, Pa stokes his fires and boils up grains for beer or works in their little garden, weeding and planting vegetables.

He covers the beds with seaweed collected from shore to help the plants grow, and has used driftwood to make a fence around it to protect as much from the wind and spray as he can. The wood has been bleached in the sun and smoothed and polished to old bones by the ocean. Barnacle shells decorate some pieces, like jewellery or medals, celebrating how far they've travelled.

Much as he moans about the work, Meg thinks Pa is quite proud of the garden, and it does produce many of the vegetables Meg uses for cooking.

By late afternoon the Alehouse becomes hectic as the longshoremen, farm labourers and fishermen finish work. Meg is busy serving beer and vitals to the hungry men.

Of William Rufus and the excise men, there is no sign.

'Happen they were away down the coast last night,' Pa says. 'Neville Sharp told me that a boat had foundered on the Bright Rock.'

'Wreckers?' Meg asks. It is unusual for boats to ground when the weather is good. There have been no severe storms for a while.

Her father shrugs.

Meg purses her lips. Smuggling is one thing. The only person harmed is the King with the loss of duty. But wreckers who lure ships onto the rocks and kill the whole crew and any passengers so they can rightly claim that no one was alive on board to own the cargo are in a different league.

One morning Meg climbs the ladder, carrying a tankard of willow bark tea for Nat and finds Harry standing by a thin bit of roof thatch, his eye against the straw, peering out to the estuary. He has barely left his brother for the past few days.

'He's sleeping,' Meg says, looking down at Nat. 'Will you not come down and take a break?'

Nat's breathing is better. Meg thinks the fever has broken but there is still a sheen to his face, and he is the colour of dandelion down and so weak he could blow away as easily. He has slept for days, sometimes as still as a post and at other times writhing and turning and muttering in his dreams.

Meg puts the tankard down near Nat, but far enough away that he won't knock it if he turns over and goes back to the ladder. She glances again at Harry, and he reluctantly follows her down. Jip is delighted to see this person that has been out of his reach and jumps up excitedly.

'Jip! Down,' Meg scolds and leads the way down the steep stairs. She takes Harry through the kitchen to the yard outside where he accepts the chance to wash in the trough and use Pa's razor.

'I can wash your shirt,' Meg tells him, indicating his bloodstained front. 'It'll dry fast enough in the sun. Go through to the garden, Pa is working.'

Jip follows Harry about, interested in the visitor. Meg is surprised. He is usually loyal to her alone.

She takes Harry's shirt, still warm from his body, and fills the wooden pail from the pump. She scrubs the linen in the water several times, beating it with the paddle, before throwing it over the hedge to dry.

She can hear Harry and her Pa's voices carry from the other side.

'Josiah has arranged another landing,' her father says. 'Two days' time, while the moon is still low. The excise men have been busy down the coast these last few nights so happen we'll be left in peace.'

'But Nat . . .' Harry begins.

'Only one boat,' her father growls. 'We don't need a full complement and Nat will be fine here with Meg. She'll watch over him if you need.'

Meg doesn't wait to hear Harry's reply. This is a conversation she isn't meant to hear. Is one boat unusual or is Josiah squeezing in an extra run?

Still puzzling it over, she goes inside and climbs the stairs and the ladder to check on Nat. As the boards creak under her weight his eyes flicker open.

Meg's head jerks back in surprise.

'You're awake. How do you feel?' she asks.

Nat croaks something in reply and licks his dry lips. Meg lifts the tankard of willow bark tea to his mouth, and he takes a few sips before pushing it away with a grimace.

'I know it tastes bad, but Mistress Cooper sent it for your fever. It's better if you'll drink it.'

Nat screws his face up in reply and Meg remembers he is little more than a child.

'Where's Harry?' he asks instead. 'Did he get away?'

For a moment Meg is confused, uncertain what he is talking about but then she remembers the boy must be remembering the night of the smuggling run. He may not have remembered anything since.

She nods.

'He carried you here with my Pa. He's been here by your side all the while and has only this minute stepped out for some sunlight.'

'What happened?' Nat asks.

'The excise men shot you,' Meg tells him. 'Harry got the musket ball out. You've been asleep for a few days. He'll want to know you're awake. I'll fetch him.'

Nat grins at her, his face so hollow it is ghoulish and Meg hurries down the ladder and stairs.

'Harry, Harry?' she calls running through the kitchen towards the yard and straight into William Rufus.

'Who is Harry?' William asks, putting an arm across the doorway to bar her way. 'I thought it was only you and old man Parton here.'

He leans in closely so that Meg has a fine view of his scar, a raised red puckered line ending at his lip and can smell sweat on him.

Meg feels her cheeks colour as thoughts whirl through her mind.

'Harry is family. Distant family,' she says numbly. 'Come to stay a while. To help Pa.'

'To help him with what?' William asks, his eyes narrowing. 'Business?'

'At the moment he's helping with the garden,' Meg says loudly, as Pa and Harry come round the corner to the yard. 'Pa's getting on and between the brewing and running the Alehouse and all, the garden gets a bit neglected,' she adds for good measure.

As Pa and Harry stop abruptly and look at her thunderstruck, Meg thinks quickly.

'Harry!' she calls out in a sing-song voice. 'This is William Rufus, a revenue man. I was explaining you are staying a while to help Pa.'

Harry and Pa glance at each other and nod.

''Tis true,' Harry says. 'Summer by the estuary and to see how the brewing trade suits me.'

William does not appear convinced but there is little he can say.

He leans in a little closer to Meg.

'If your Pa is giving up,' he says. 'Giving up everything, that is, remember there is a place for you in town.'

Then he backs away from Meg and she shivers involuntarily. He lifts his hat to them all and turns away. When he is out of sight Meg grabs Harry's arm.

'Nat's awake,' she hisses. 'I said I'd call you, but then William was here and wanted to know who you were.'

'Awake, you say. Amen!' Harry says. 'I'll go to him.'

'I'll bring him up some broth shortly,' Meg says.

Harry turns and hurries towards the door when Pa calls out.

'Harry! You might want to put your shirt on. No wonder Rufus was looking at you so oddly. He was probably wondering what was going on.'

Harry grins, the first time Meg has seen him smile properly and she notices slight dimples in his cheeks. It is not all she has noticed either. He has a fine toned body, with broad shoulders. His arms, neck and face are sun tanned but she'd guess he takes off his shirt on occasion while he works.

'I didn't even think,' Harry says clapping a hand to his head and grabbing his shirt from the bushes. He pulls it over his head even though it is still damp.

Shame, Meg thinks. She is used to Pa and a variety of older working men in the Brewhouse. Harry's shapely body is a more pleasant view.

She smiles to herself as she turns back into the kitchen followed by the traitorous Jip who is still staring, longingly after Harry, and stirs the big cauldron over the fire.

As she ladles some of the broth into a tankard to take upstairs, she wonders about the conversation she overheard.

Pa hasn't been away from the Brewhouse for days so word from Josiah must have come to him here. Yet no-one she knows is called Josiah. It is not a name she recognises from those who eat and drink in The Anchor.

The message, she realises, must have been passed on from someone else, probably through several people, until it reached Pa. But who then is Josiah, and why is he such a shadowy, mystical figure? True, it is safer for him if no-one knows his identity, for then no-one can turn him in to the authorities, but for someone who barely exists he wields a great deal of power; and the local men, like Pa and Harry, are tumbling over themselves do to his bidding.

10

When Meg climbs up the ladder again, she finds Harry crouched over his brother, brushing the hair from his face.

Nat is curled on one side, his breathing even, and the slightest pink flush to his cheeks like the petals of a wild rose.

Meg raises her eyebrows to Harry.

'He was asleep when I got up here,' he tells her.

'He was awake, truly,' Meg says. 'He was disorientated. He wanted to know if you got away.'

Harry nods.

'Well, I've brought up some broth now,' Meg says. 'You have it. There is more in the kitchen, but we'll have customers in soon, so if you come down make it very quiet. I suppose now that William Rufus knows you are here you may as well be seen about.'

Harry nods again and gives her a small smile. Meg immediately feels guilty for telling him to go outside at exactly the time Nat woke.

Still, Harry must feel cleaner and fresher. She wishes there was a window in the attic she could throw open and air the roof space. Even with the holes in the thatch, the attic has become muggy and thick with sweat and fever.

She fears anyone climbing the stairs will be immediately aware there is a sick room up here, even without any unintentional noise from Harry or Nat.

'Pull the ladder up when I've gone,' she tells Harry and climbs back down to Jip, who is waiting faithfully for her at the bottom.

In the kitchen she turns her attention to preparation for the day. Bread dough is kneaded and put to rise. She makes some oatcakes on the griddle. One of the fishermen has promised her his catch today so she chops vegetables for the pot. Customers can have soup or fish fried on the skillet with a hunk of fresh bread.

Pa is still in the garden, clearing a bed and digging over ready to plant more seeds. Meg can see him from the door-way, stooping and rising and wiping his brow alternately. The garden was her mother's passion and Pa keeps it going in her memory and because Meg reminds him how good the vegetables are for meals she cooks.

A wave of love for Pa suddenly threatens to overwhelm Meg. Since Ma died it's only been the two of them, and whilst they may not share confidences as she once did with Ma, and Pa is hopeless with anything important like dresses or hairstyles, he has always been there for her and always has her back.

An icy trickle of worry runs down her spine. What would happen if Pa was caught by the excise men? She doesn't know how she'd carry on.

She hurries out to the store and digs into the apple barrel. A few wizened fruits from last year remain at the bottom.

Meg takes them into the kitchen and chops them up. Then she mixes a little flour with an egg from the hens and milk from the goat and cooks them all together in the skillet. When it's ready she calls Pa in from the garden and tells him to sit.

'What's this for, Meggie?' Pa asks, his eyes widening at the treat she's put on the table.

Meg shrugs and puts the honey on the table.

'Just . . .' she says.

Pa narrows his eyes.

'Eat,' Meg urges.

Pa spoons some honey on to his apple fritter. He uses a tin spoon and cuts a big slice. He grins as he swallows.

'This is lovely,' he says, chopping the next mouthful. 'Just like your Ma used to make.'

'We could plant more apple trees,' Meg says.

'Wind,' Pa says, through a mouthful of fritter. 'They won't grow to full size with the salt here. Nothing grows as it should. Not like it would in the village.'

'Except the cabbages,' Meg says with a grin.

'Yes, well, thank goodness for cabbage,' Pa says, scraping round his plate with the spoon and smacking his lips. 'That was grand, Meg. I'll get tidied up outside. People will be in soon.'

'Pa,' Meg says slowly. 'Who is Josiah?'

Pa looks up sharply, the comfortable smile gone from his face, a pinched, hunted look replacing it.

'Don't you worry about that, Meg. Stay out of it.'

'But who is he, Pa? I don't know anyone of that name from around here.'

'That's good.' Pa's voice is waspish, and the good mood produced by the sweet treat is gone from the kitchen as he stomps out back to the garden.

The atmosphere between them remains tense for the rest of the day. Customers begin drifting into the Alehouse as the tide changes and boats leave the staithes.

First in is Bert, a balding man, stooped from years of carrying goods up and down the gangplanks to the boats docked at the staithes. When Meg was little and walking into the village with her mother, they would stop and watch as the nimble-footed men practically danced up the wooden planks carrying sacks of coal or bales of wool on their heads or clasping barrels of fish to their chests.

Meg has an idea that Bert is also involved in the night business. He is very thick with her father and certainly used to hauling cargo.

She notices no difference in his demeanour. He sits as usual, on a stool near the fire, hugging his tankard to his chest. Years ago, Meg remembers, he had a family and several children, but they all died of fever one winter, and after that Bert practically moved into the Alehouse, making it his second home.

Mal brings Meg in a basket of fish, which she cleans and guts at the pump in the yard. The scales fly everywhere and the odour clings to her hands and apron.

But the catch is fresh and smells good as she fries it, so good it sells out quickly. However, when Meg goes into the bar with platters of food, Pa doesn't meet

her eye and she has the impression conversations are halted until she has gone.

Meg is quite glad when the evening is
over, and Pa shows the last customers out
of the door. She takes a wooden platter
of bread and cheese up the stairs with
her as Pa puts the wooden bar across the
door.

Jip looks interested as she stands below
the attic trap and calls softly to Harry.

'Harry, I have some food. How is Nat?'

The board moves and Meg stands
back as Harry lowers the ladder down.
He reaches down and Meg passes up the
plate, then she climbs up herself.

'How is he?' she asks.

Harry shakes his head.

'He hasn't woken again.'

Meg grimaces.

Now Harry blames her, too. She's put
both him and Pa out today.

A candle flickers between them as
Harry sits on the floor and eagerly takes
a bite of the bread. At least his appetite
has returned, Meg thinks. It must be
because Nat is at least looking better.

'As soon as I can move him, we'll be off,' Harry says through a mouthful of bread, jerking his hand behind towards Nat.

'I don't think that will be for a while yet,' Meg tells him. 'He might have woken but he'll be as weak as a kitten for a while yet and he probably shouldn't walk on that leg. No more night business for him.'

'Aye, well,' Harry looks down at the plate. His face is in shadow, and Meg can't tell if he is happy or disappointed by that.

'Who is Josiah?' she asks suddenly. 'How did you meet him?'

Harry looks up. His eyes are wide and dark in the dim light.

'I've never met him,' he says. 'Word comes around about work from different people. Someone always knows when the next landing will be and how many people are needed. Payment comes the same way, from one hand to another.'

'But doesn't he appear at night for the landing to oversee —'

Harry shakes his head vigorously.

'No. Not that I know of. I don't know who he is and so wouldn't recognise him if he were there. It's a small and regular gang who work and if someone is new there'll be someone to vouch for them and show them the ropes. Not that it's tricky. Not if you've been round boats a bit.'

'But —' Meg begins.

Harry puts a hand on her arm. His touch is firm, and Meg feels blood flood through her.

'Don't, Meg. Don't ask. Don't get involved. They are bad people. They haul you in like a fisherman with a net. You can't get away. The outcome will never be good.'

He drops his gaze from her face to the dusty floor.

'Why don't you get out, then?' Meg says.

'To do that I'd have to go a long way away, where their clutches don't reach. I don't think Nat is ready for that yet. But I'm saving. One day I intend to get us away and set up a business where I can work as my own boss and not be at someone's beck and call.'

Meg looks at him and this time he does meet her eye. She feels the stuffing has been knocked out of her. Harry has only been staying in the attic a few days and she's had very few conversations with him but the thought that he might go far away and she won't get to know him better leaves her with a hollow feeling.

11

The following morning Meg checks on Harry and Nat.

'He's been awake. For a bit,' Harry says. 'But he keeps falling asleep again.'

'That's good,' Meg says. 'His body is healing.'

She isn't quite sure if this is true, but she feels the need to give Harry hope. Nat certainly looks better. He is still very thin and hollowed out but there are spots of colour in his cheeks, and his breathing is even and no longer creaking like a broken cart.

'I'll get you some gruel and then I'm away to church,' she tells him. 'If I don't go it will appear odd. Pa will be here, but I expect he will be in the Brewhouse.'

When they have broken fast, Meg kisses her father goodbye, ties on her bonnet, and heads off along the dyke towards the village. Jip watches her go, a mournful expression on his face as if she might be deserting him for ever.

Meg used to be taken in by this, but she knows now he'll go and find Pa and settle down with him for the hours she's gone.

'Meg!' Eliza is waiting for her by the lych gate. As usual, she is impeccably dressed, her frock having a large white collar, which exaggerates her dark hair. A panel of a contrasting fabric has been inserted in the front of her dress and the waist is drawn in tightly giving the impression of wide hips and a small bustle.

Her dark hair pokes from beneath her bonnet and curls charmingly round her face.

'Beautiful,' Meg says admiringly.

Eliza twirls around for Meg to see.

'I took the panel from an old dress of Ma's,' she says. 'None of it is new.'

Meg shakes her head and looks down at her own blue woollen frock that she has been wearing for best all year. It is a little short to avoid the mud on the walk but still it is splattered. She feels hopelessly inadequate compared to her friend.

'You're clever,' she says, taking Eliza's arm. 'Now,' she lowers her voice and moves closer. 'Tell me, have you come across someone called Josiah in the village? I've been racking my brains, but I cannot think of anyone.'

'Josiah? You mean the Squire?' Eliza asks, tilting her head and pausing.

Meg claps a hand to her forehead.

'The Squire! Why did I never think of him? Of course. I think of him only as Squire Padgett.'

'What do you want with him?' Eliza asks. 'He doesn't mix with the likes of us.'

'You and your mother go to the big house?' Meg asks.

Eliza nods.

'Of course, whenever his wife or the girls need dresses sewn or alterations done, although they have a lady's maid who can —'

'Yes,' Meg cuts her off. 'What does the Squire do?'

Eliza draws back a little and looks at her.

'He's away a lot. I believe he sits in Parliament and he's a justice of the peace so there are the courts to attend to. I've very seldom seen him. Why?'

Meg presses her lips together but sees the look on Eliza's face and knows she has peaked her friend's interest.

'I've heard the name Josiah mentioned,' she admits. 'In connection with the night business.'

Eliza hisses as she inhales a breath sharply. She shakes her head.

'Not the Squire, Meg. You've got the wrong person there. He's quite above anything like that. Why, they have money to do whatever they want. They don't need more.'

Meg frowns.

'That is precisely the sort of person who maybe involved. Where did his money come from, eh?'

Eliza removes Meg's hand from her arm.

'No,' she says. 'I won't believe it. They

are a good family. Mistress Padgett delivers relief to the bereaved. They treat their staff well. I am treated well when I go to work there.'

'That means nothing,' Meg says. 'Except they can afford to be generous.'

'If money was that important, they wouldn't be generous, though, would they?' Eliza asks with what Meg thinks is exasperating logic.

She has found someone with the name Josiah. It must be the Squire running the night business. Who better to know the routes of the ships and organise with foreigners for deliveries?

'Come,' Eliza says. 'We'll be late if we tarry here.'

Meg has hardly noticed but the stream of people entering the church has dried up.

They hurry along the path, a crow bouncing on the ground in front of them and another watching, perching darkly on a leaning gravestone. The door creaks and Meg feels her face heat as they slip into the wooden pews at the back.

Meg wishes they'd been quicker and got a seat nearer the front of the church where she would have a better view of the Squire and his family in the most prestigious seats. As it is she cannot see round the heads and bonnets to those seated nearest the altar.

Her attention wanders as the minister, the Reverend Green, booms out his sermon. Next to her, Eliza is nodding in agreement, but Meg catches only the occasional word and although Reverend Green speaks for at least half an hour she has honestly no recollection of what he has been saying.

She watches his balding head at the front of the church bobbing with the intensity of his address and his mouth opening and closing like one of the puppets operated by strings, she's seen at the summer fayre.

She stares up at the rafters of the small church. A sparrow is trapped inside and sits trembling on a beam as Reverend Green's voice echoes thunderously around, while the light from candles in the sconces throws shadows about the church as the flames flicker in the draught.

At last, the minister appears to have run out of energy, and there is a call for prayer. People stand and bow their heads and Meg can no longer see anyone beyond those in front of herself and Eliza.

She watches as the congregation file out of the church led by Reverend Green. Squire Padgett, his wife and three daughters follow close behind. There is no-one else of his status in the village and everyone else falls in behind, leaving a respectful distance. Outside the porch, Reverend Green stops to greet people.

First is Squire Padgett. Meg watches as they shake hands, craning her head to see them clearly. Squire Padgett stands tall, sure of his position. He has an open face, well-nourished but not overweight.

Reverend Green is short by comparison, and his complexion is not good. His cheeks are a mass of broken veins, and his eyes are dull.

'Come away,' Eliza tugs her arm and

hisses at her.

Meg shakes her off.

The Squire's wife also shakes the Reverend Green's hand and the three girls, only one of whom is old enough for long skirts, shuffle and tussle with each other as they wait impatiently for their parents. At last, the Squire finishes what he was saying and the family walk away to the lane where their carriage awaits.

Other members of the congregation gather round Reverend Green, but Meg is still watching the Squire as he helps his wife and children into the open carriage before climbing in himself.

He appears a family man, concerned and patient, but that does not exclude him from the cutthroat business of smuggling, at least not in Meg's eyes.

'No,' Eliza says to her. 'Definitely not. It feels wrong.'

'But who else can it be,' Meg hisses back. 'No-one else is named Josiah. You said yourself you knew no one else. It must be him.'

Eliza shakes her head.

'You're wrong,' she says.

'I'll have to prove it,' Meg says.

'Meg, you're so stubborn!'

'It's ruining lives, Eliza. It's ruining Pa's life and mine.'

Eliza gives her an exasperated look and turns away, beginning a conversation with Mr Bracken from the shop.

Meg clenches her fists and grinds her teeth. Surely Eliza can see that the village is better cleared of this trade. It endangers too many lives. She thinks of poor Nat, upstairs in the attic, his face as pale as the barn owl that sometimes swoops over the estuary, his limbs as thin as those of the wading birds that inhabit the shallows.

Eliza wouldn't be so callous if she knew, Meg is sure, but still, she is not happy as she walks home past the staithes. Only one ship is moored, and a single deck hand is scrubbing the boards with limited interest. The doors to the warehouse are shut and the smithy is quiet.

Jip bounds out of the Alehouse excitedly as Meg is still several hundred yards from home. He always senses when she is near and unless Pa has shut him inside, he rushes out to greet her. He dances around her as if she's been gone for weeks rather than hours.

She bends down to pat him.

'Did you miss me, boy?'

'He did.'

Meg looks up sharply.

Harry has approached without her hearing.

'He's been waiting by the door of the Brewhouse, listening for you, although I don't know how he heard you over your father's whistling.'

Meg flinches.

'Pa's been known to clear the Alehouse on a night when he's in his cups and decides to sing,' she says. 'That's why we often have Alan come with his accordion to play a tune. I have to watch Pa doesn't drink too much.'

'Oh, he wasn't drinking,' Harry assures her. 'I think he was feeling cheerful. Nat has been awake and talking. It's been good to hear him, and I believe the news cheered your Pa.'

Meg smiles. The news has cheered her too.

'It would,' she says.

Harry shuffles his feet and spins his hat in his hands. He appears about to say something more when a shout comes from the Alehouse.

'Meggie! You're home. The men are starving here!'

12

Meg takes off her bonnet and ties an apron around herself. Her dress might not be as smart as Eliza's but there is no point in ruining it unnecessarily. As she thinks of Eliza a lump rises in her throat.

They've never argued before, not to this extent, and she still feels Eliza is wrong. The night business must be stopped before lives are lost. If the Squire is involved . . .

'Can I help?'

A voice interrupts her thoughts, and she looks up into the grey eyes of Harry. He has followed her inside.

His skin is paler, Meg notices. Being inside this past week has given him the look of the sick bed himself.

Meg switches her thoughts from Eliza to the kitchen and looks around for a moment.

'Eggs,' she says. 'I need the eggs collected and the goat needs milking.'

Harry's eyebrows rise almost to his hairline.

'You've never milked a goat?' she asks.

'Ma had some hens but we'd no goat,' he says.

'Well, it's a good time to learn,' Meg says. ''Tis a life skill.'

She grabs the empty milk pail from the corner of the kitchen and the milking stool and strides out of the door.

The nanny is tethered in a small field. Meg rattles the pail and climbs over the fence. The nanny comes trotting towards her and is rewarded by a crust of bread from Meg's pocket.

While the goat is busy eating Meg shortens the rope about her neck and fastens it to the fence. She places the stool in position and gestures to Harry to sit.

He appears huge and finely balanced on the small seat, but the legs hold and Meg shows him how to squeeze and pull on the nanny's teats. As she does it a fine jet of milk hits the bucket. She is aware of his body warmth as she leans close.

'You try.'

Harry's big hands grasp the teat, and he appears to mimic Meg's actions. The goat, however, is not impressed. She stamps a foot.

'Gently,' Meg cautions.

Harry takes a deep breath and tries again.

This time the nanny looks round, her glassy eyes fixed on Harry before she lifts a rear leg and aims a good kick at him.

'Owww!' Harry jumps up, spilling the pail and rubbing his leg.

Meg bites her lip to stop herself laughing. She isn't sure which is funnier, the look of triumph on the nanny's face or the anger on Harry's.

'I'm sorry,' she splutters, holding a hand to her mouth to hide her laughter. 'I thought she'd be fine. Let me do it.'

Meg straightens the stool and the bucket, runs a hand along the goat's back and begins the milking. Harry, meanwhile, leans back against the fence, scowling at the goat and rubbing his leg.

''Tis not as bad as Nat,' Meg says.

'True,' Harry says, straightening up. 'Very true. Nat has taken his pain well, and it is to my shame I am making a fuss.'

'I expect it hurt,' Meg says. 'She has sharp hooves and she's quick to temper. We lost a goat the winter last and have not replaced it yet. I believe she is lonely.'

In five minutes, Meg is satisfied the goat is comfortable again. She picks up the stool and the pail. Harry steps over the fence and takes the pail from her so Meg can climb over, too.

'Would you collect the eggs?' she asks. 'It'll be cabbage and eggs for lunch.'

Back in the kitchen she shreds a cabbage and puts the skillet over the fire with some mutton fat in it. Then she lets the cabbage fry and slices a few shreds of ham into it from the joint hanging from the ceiling.

When Harry appears with half a dozen eggs, she breaks them into another pan and fries them quickly.

She dishes up a bowl for Nat and Harry first and Harry takes them off upstairs. Then she calls Pa from the Brewhouse.

They sit in the kitchen with their lunch. Sundays are quieter in the Ale house since the staithes are barely working and most folk go to the church or to chapel. Although the door is open the cooking has created a fug in the low kitchen and Meg watches dust motes dancing in the hazy sunlight.

She stretches out her legs under the table and leans back against the kitchen wall. She likes the slower feel to the day.

Her eyelids are heavy, and Meg is near sleep when Jip scrabbles to his feet beside her and Harry appears from the stairs.

'Thank you,' he says, handing back the two bowls. Meg looks. One is empty and the other half eaten.

'Sorry.' Harry shrugs. 'Nat didn't want it all.'

'You finish it, then,' Meg says.

Harry glances at her and then wolfs down the rest of it.

Jip gives a big sigh and sinks down on the ground.

Meg laughs.

'You've disappointed Jip,' she says.

'He thought the leftovers were for him.'

'Sorry, Jip.' Harry puts the bowl on the table and scratches the dog's head. Jip's tail thumps on the floor.

'I thought I might go for a walk along the coast,' he says, looking up at Meg from under his eyebrows. 'Would you and Jip like to come? Unless you have work,' he adds hurriedly.

'She's no work,' Pa says, getting to his feet and heading to the doorway. 'Sundays are quiet until later and then not so many want food.'

He goes out, leaving Meg embarrassed that he's spoken for her.

'Jip would like a walk,' she says after a moment. 'Now?'

Harry nods, so Meg takes off her apron, glad her frock is still clean, and grabs her bonnet from the hook. They set off along the coast away from the river estuary. A well-trodden path lies behind the sand dunes which rise above the beach.

'So how is Nat?' Meg asks as she throws a stick for Jip to chase.

'He is awake a little more,' Harry says. 'But each time he eats or talks a while he must sleep again.'

'He's still weak,' Meg says. 'It will take him time to recover. And your leg?' She nods at the leg the nanny kicked.

Harry laughs.

'Wounded pride,' he says. 'I'll not be felled by a goat.'

They walk along in silence for a bit. Jip brings sticks to be thrown and bounds into the shallows after them.

'I should go back to work,' Harry says. 'We can't be beholden to you any longer.'

Meg shrugs.

'I don't think Nat can be moved yet. I'm sure Pa would appreciate help, though. Can you thatch? Or fix shutters? Pa never seems to have time for these things and as you can see the Ale house is near falling down.'

Harry's face lights up.

'I can do the shutters,' he says. 'If your Pa has some tools. Never done a roof, but how hard can it be?'

Meg smiles at him.

'I'm sure that would be a fair exchange,' she says and feels herself warm inside with the thought that Harry might stay.

'How far away to you live?' she asks.

Harry points further along the coast.

'We're way in that direction,' he says. 'We lodge in Culham.'

Meg nods, though she's never been to Culham, but she's heard speak of it. There is a fishing community and several of the longshoremen come from there.

'It is nice?' she asks.

Harry shrugs.

'I like it here,' he says. 'The Anchor has a good atmosphere. Like a large family.'

Meg pouts, thinking of the nights when fights break out and the customers are not minded to tend to their manners. She would love to get away.

'It is full time,' she says. 'Never a day off.'

'True,' Harry says. 'All the more reason to stay out this afternoon.'

He leaves the path and works his way through the dunes until he gets on to the beach. Meg follows him and watches as Harry picks up a pebble, weighs it in his hand and skims it out across the sea. It bounces once, twice, up to five times, each time breaking the surface into sparkling drops. Jip stands at the shore, barking.

Meg laughs.

'I can do better than that!' she says, searching for her own stone.

Meg stands sideways on to the ocean and holding her pebble between her thumb and first two fingers, releases it low across the water. She is cheered to see it splash once, twice, three times before falling into the water.

'It wasn't a great stone,' she says, laughing and searching for another.

Harry lets go another that skips five times. Meg's next also skips five times.

As he goes to throw the next, she stands in front of him and throws hers first.

'No! Not fair,' Harry cries putting an arm round her neck from behind and pulling her close to him. He attempts to throw his stone but is unbalanced by her weight.

Meg is laughing and very aware of the warmth of Harry's body against her back.

'I win!' she calls gleefully.

'I don't think that was fair,' Harry says, gripping her tighter. 'I believe you should be dunked for that!'

'No!' Meg cries but she is laughing as Harry picks her up and carries her down to the water's edge. Jip prances along beside him, barking at them both.

'Shall I? Shall I?' Harry asks holding her out over the shallows. 'What do you think, Jip?'

Meg wriggles in his arms and Harry pulls her back towards his body. As she looks up into his face, the world seems to tilt. Harry leans forward towards her but stops suddenly and hastily puts her down in a sandy patch.

'Sorry,' he says. 'I shouldn't have presumed.'

Meg feels her face flush, not just from the effort of laughing. She smiles and brushes herself down unnecessarily to hide her confusion. A line has been crossed, or almost crossed, and she can't help but feel a little disappointed Harry's playfulness did not go further.

13

They walk back towards The Anchor in silence. Meg avoids thinking about what almost happened. It was just the moment, she tells herself. Why would someone like Harry, who has his whole life ahead of him, be interested in her, tied up at the Ale house as she is.

But as the Alehouse comes into view, squat and solid on the flat wide landscape, Harry stops walking and turns to her.

'Thank you for this afternoon,' he says. 'It was nice to do something fun.'

It is then Meg realises she hasn't thought about Nat or the night business either while they've been out. It has been relaxing.

She smiles up at Harry and is about to tell him that she has enjoyed the afternoon, too, when they are interrupted.

'Harry, Harry!' Pa's voice reaches them along the sea front, startling the wading birds on the beach. 'We're needed. Tonight!'

★ ★ ★

The evening in The Anchor passes as most others. Meg prepares food and serves while her father pours tankards of ale and listens to tales of woe from customers, encouraging them to drown their sorrows.

As the bar quietens down Meg takes herself upstairs. She climbs up into the warm attic. Night has fallen but it is not fully dark, and splashes of light break through the thatched roof.

She looks down at Nat.

'How is he?' she asks.

'Good,' Harry says.

'Are you going out tonight?' Meg asks.

She feels Harry stiffen beside her.

'It's dangerous,' she says. 'Think about Nat. What will he do if you are injured?'

'I have no choice. If Josiah needs help, we have to go. It's dangerous not to.'

Meg feels her nostrils flare.

'How does he wield so much power over you all when no-one knows who he is?' she hisses.

'To upset him brings retribution, as much as the excise men can bring,' Harry says. 'If I don't appear, at least not without good reason, Nat's life could be in danger. It's the same for your Pa.' He shrugs apologetically.

Meg thins her lips. She hasn't realised Josiah's power is so strong, or the pressure he exerts on Pa involves her and the Alehouse. She'd thought Pa worked for the money.

'Those involved know too much about the operations,' Harry continues. 'Once in, you're in for life.'

Meg goes back down the ladder and lies on her pallet. Her mind is racing and her body fizzes with the injustice. Even if anyone wanted to get out of the night business it sounds as if it is made impossible.

At last, she hears Pa climbing the stairs, with a slow, heavy tread. He's tired, she thinks, and he's no longer young. The night business is a young man's game. She wishes there was something she could do to help, but other than take as much of the daily work from him she didn't know what.

The tell-tale creaking of the stairs wakes her some time later. She gets up and stands close to the window. Moving the shutter slightly she can see two silhouettes striding out along the sea path in the direction of Culham. It will be minutes before they are out of sight.

Meg makes a quick decision. She pulls on her stockings, petticoats and frock. She lifts her dark cloak from the nail and creeps downstairs.

She has no fear of the dark, but her stomach is hard and she feels her adrenaline spiking. The waves, which are little more than ripples, sound especially loud, and however she tries to stay quiet, her footsteps seemed to thud on the hardened ground.

Meg has no idea how far she needs to go. She pulls her cloak tighter and keeps her head down. Ahead she knows there is a path off to the left, away from the sea, that is a short cut to the village, cutting off the estuary corner with The Anchor and the staithes.

She reckons there is a good chance the activity will be near there since carts can be brought down close to the sea.

She stops before she reaches the spot and finds some tussocky grass to squat down beside. The sand is chilly, and Meg shuffles about until she's hollowed herself out a depression to rest in.

She sits for what seems like ages, wondering if she's made a mistake, if no-one is coming, or the meeting place is in some other direction. She looks round but can see nothing except the distant dark outlines of trees and a few stars glittering through the darkness of the sky.

Suddenly she glimpses a flash of light out to sea, not far off the coast.

A flash from a lantern in the dunes ahead answers the light and then, seemingly from nowhere, half a dozen dark shapes stand up and swarm towards the beach.

Meg's mouth falls open. She had no idea she is so close to the smugglers. If she'd gone another fifty yards, she'd have been in amongst them, tripping over legs and feet. They have hidden themselves so well amongst the dunes she had no knowledge of them.

Meg watches a two-masted wooden boat appear out of the darkness, poled by men with long sticks towards the shore.

She clenches her fists as the men stride into the shallows and snatch barrels and large packages from hands on the boat. A rowing boat appears from the darkness and some of the barrels are loaded on to that, but most are carried at a jolting run up the beach, through the dunes to two carts that have pulled up on the path.

The men, bent under the weight of their loads, all know exactly what to do. Meg can see no-one in charge giving orders, and it is all carried out in silence, with only the odd grunt or curse carrying in the night air.

Meg sighs quietly. What was she thinking? That Squire Padgett would be here himself overseeing operations? She kicks at the ground, barely able to keep her impatience at bay. She won't find out who is in charge tonight. Not this way.

She gazes off into the distance, vaguely aware of the boat being emptied. The operation is slick, and it does not take that long. As soon as the first cart is full, it trundles away towards the village and the next is filled. When she hears the wheels of that creaking away, she is almost ready to stand up and make her way back to The Anchor.

But before she can move, she feels the ground beneath her shake and in seconds she hears the hollow thud of a horse's hooves on the path.

The excise men.

She wonders whether to cry out and warn the smugglers, but she quickly realises that they have heard the sound, too, and the boat is being hurriedly poled back out into deeper water. Most of the men have melted away. Only the rowing boat remains and three men on the shore who toss the last barrels into it and leap in after.

Two men sit in the middle and take an oar while the others crouch low beneath the gunwale. The whole thing is low in the water, what with the barrels and packages and three of them aboard. It is slow to pull away and Meg holds her breath, willing it out of sight.

The sound of the horse's hooves is now almost on top of her, and Meg hears a whinny. She drags her cloak over her head and crouches down in her sandy nest as the horse pulls up and grit is flicked over her.

She risks a last quick glance at the rowing boat which, barely above the water, is gradually pulling away into the dark, then the night seems to explode around her as a shot is fired, deafening her.

14

Meg stuffs her fist in her mouth to stop herself crying out. The explosions are so loud and so powerful and so close, that the air shudders around her, like an intense storm. She can't imagine what it must feel like to be hit by a musket shot.

She can hear William's horse stamping the ground as he tries to keep it still.

'Fire, fire!' he shouts, and there is scrabbling and grunts as his men struggle to reload their guns.

It is a minute or two before more shots sound. In the interval Meg strains her ears to hear the rowing boat, but between the noise of excise men working on their muskets, William's horse stamping about and the waves on the shore, she can no longer hear the creak of the oars, and she is hopeful the smugglers have got away.

'It's too dark, Sir. I can't see 'em,' one of William's men says.

'Keep trying!' William barks. 'And somebody reload my gun.'

Meg hears the horse's hooves move along the path away from her and she opens her eyes. She hears a flint struck and, peering from under her cloak, she can see a lantern has been lit. Now she is completely trapped as they will surely see her move.

There is a scrape of metal and the rustling of clothing and bags and then a snap, which she presumes is William's gun being primed.

'Give it to me,' he says. His voice has the same snarl to it that Jip has if he is guarding a bone from another dog.

Meg gives an involuntary shiver just as the gun explodes again.

'Bah!' William's voice is flat and oozes disappointment. 'It's too dark to see. Right, back to the village. Maybe we can catch them unloading the stuff.'

His horse whinnies and the hooves shuffle as Meg imagines he is turning towards the village to head along the short cut. She hopes the smugglers have had time to get away and the carts are back in the barns and stables where they should be.

She listens. Gradually the sound of the horse and men's boots on the path fade, and she is left with the whoosh of the sea on the beach and the occasional rattle as a stone moves.

Even though she can no longer hear William or his men, Meg stays where she is, covered by her cloak until the peace of night blankets the coast. At last she feels brave enough to uncover herself and look around.

She is surprised she can see hardly anything. Whilst she has been hiding, a sea fret has blown in and white swirling mist like the smoke from a hundred clay pipes covers the ground as far as she can see.

Oddly, it lies very low so that as Meg stands, she can see over it. She uses her feet, testing each step until she finds her way back on to the shore path. Even then, though she knows it well enough in the daytime, she takes each step carefully.

The journey is slow and made slower as Meg starts at noises, imagining William Rufus returning to check on The Anchor. She wouldn't put it past him, if can't find anything in the village. At one point she starts as she sees a pair of glassy, green eyes staring at her, but when she blinks, they are gone.

And as for Pa and Harry, she has no idea where they are. Did they go with the carts to the village? Were they part of the group of men who slipped away like wraiths as the excise men appeared, or were they the ones who jumped into the boat and desperately rowed away. The man who took the oar was big and strong like Harry.

Eventually she reaches The Anchor and hurries round to the yard to open the back door. The bar is not across the door so Pa and Harry must still be out.

'Come on,' she says to Jip, and they climb the stairs.

Meg is tired, bone weary tired, and she drops down on her pallet to pull off her boots and stockings. She doesn't even bother to hang her frock and petticoats from the nail but leaves them in a heap on the floor.

Jip lies close to her as she pulls the blanket over herself.

She expects to fall asleep immediately, but she is listening for her father. The night wears on but Meg cannot sleep. She turns over and Jip sighs as if she is keeping him awake.

Meg tosses and turns. Not only is it Pa she is worried about now but Harry, too. In the end, she takes her blanket and climbs the ladder into the attic. Nat is asleep, breathing peacefully. Meg lies beside him, feeling his warmth.

The sound of footsteps on the stairs wakes her with a jolt and she sits sharply upright, wondering for a moment where she is. The pinpricks of light through the roof tell her that dawn is coming and from the whispers below she guesses both Pa and Harry are back.

She takes her blanket and wraps it round herself and climbs down the ladder.

'Meggie!'

Pa looks haggard in the grey light. His face is pewter coloured and there are dark bags under his eyes. His clothing is wet, and his hair is wild and sticking out from his head. She can smell sweat and salt on him.

Harry doesn't look much better. His clothing is sticking to him, and he appears exhausted.

Meg gives them a pained look.

'Is Nat all right?' Harry asks.

'He's fine,' Meg says. 'He's asleep.'

Pa meets her eye.

'Had a bit of bother,' he says. 'We didn't mean to be out so long.'

Meg swallows and clenches her fists around her thumbs. She wants to shout at them, ask them how she feels, knowing they might not be home one night.

But instead, she turns sharply on her heel and goes into her room so they won't see her bottom lip quivering. From outside she hears Pa and Harry whispering.

'We'll have to let Josiah know,' Pa says. 'I'll send a message along later today.

Meanwhile best grab an hour's sleep so we are up and working if Rufus should appear.'

Meg grabs the blanket and pulls it closer as she remembers the explosions the musket made and how close it had been.

She falls asleep again wondering where Pa and Harry have been.

15

They all wake later than usual, although Meg is downstairs, sweeping out the bar and laying fresh sawdust, trimming the lamps, stoking the fires and collecting stray tankards before she hears movement from above.

'Meggie, love. It's a beautiful day.'

Her father stands in the doorway of the kitchen looking out at the yard and the sea, scratching his stomach beneath his waistcoat.

The waistcoat is one Eliza embroidered with anchors especially for him, Meg sees, and she feels a twinge of remorse.

She shouldn't have argued with Eliza or left their conversation unmended. They've always been there for each other and the night business, which, after all, neither of them is involved in, shouldn't have come between them.

Pa doesn't wear the waistcoat often.

'For best,' he said once when she had asked about it.

The sunlight pouring into the kitchen shows up cobwebs and dust and Meg has an urge to clean and tidy and set everything to rights.

'Sit, Pa,' she says. 'I'll get you some porridge, then I'm going to tidy the kitchen.'

Her father shuffles over to the stools and waits patiently as Meg throws some oats in the pan and puts it over the fire. She bites her tongue so as not to ask him about last night.

Just as he has finished scraping his bowl, there are more footsteps coming down the stairs.

'I'm sorry.' Harry holds up his hands. 'I didn't mean to sleep so late. It was Nat who woke me. He is anxious to come down. He is bored and wants to try walking.'

He looks between Meg and her father.

'Surely,' Pa says. 'Perhaps he can sit out a bit and then come in the Brewhouse with me, out of sight, in case we should have a visit from the excise men.

'We've explained your presence but someone who is obviously injured will draw more attention than we need.'

'Excellent.' Harry beams at them both, and Meg's resolve to keep him at a distance wavers. 'I'll fetch him down.'

Pa goes to help, and Jip follows him while Meg puts more oats on to cook.

She can hear them above and slow steady feet on the stairs and then Nat appears in the kitchen heavily supported by Harry. He is pale, his skin white and thin, ghostly. He blinks quickly at the sunlight that has made a rectangular shape on the earth-packed floor.

A smile splits his face.

''Tis nice to see something other than the thatch,' he says.

Meg smiles back.

'Sit yourself down,' she says. 'I've made porridge.'

She puts a bowl in front of Harry and Nat and pushes the salt pot and the honey jar across the table to them.

'Can you walk?' Meg asks.

'Not really,' he admits.

'Then you must stay out of the way,' Meg says. ''Tis likely we'll have a visit from the excise men, and William Rufus will be on the lookout for anyone injured.'

'We can sit you in the garden for a bit, then we'll put you in the Brewhouse where I'll be working,' Pa says. 'Bring him out when you're ready, Harry. I'm going to dig over some garden first and then I'll be inside.'

Harry nods.

'I'll help you with the garden. Then I thought I'd go along the beach and find some likely wood. Meg said the shutters needed work.'

Pa looks up in surprise.

'Yes, well, yes, they do.'

'And the roof, Pa,' Meg says. ''Tis in a dreadful state.'

Pa rubs a hand along his chin.

'I'll ask Amos if he can get some straw. I'm sorry, I've neglected the place of late.'

He looks sad and despondent and

Meg's shoulders slump. How can she remain distant from him when he needs her to keep him going?

She knows he still misses Ma terribly and she organised the upkeep of the place and bullied Pa into doing the work.

'If you get the straw, Harry says he'll have a go at fixing the roof. 'Tis the best offer we've got, so make sure you remember.'

Pa gives her a nod and beetles out of the door.

Harry is grinning, dimples denting his cheeks, and his eyes dancing with delight.

'Right, Nat. Let's get you outside.'

Meg busies herself cleaning the kitchen. She brushes down the shelves, sorts the bunches of dried herbs she has hanging from the ceiling and sweeps the floor. She takes a rag and washes the window and then does the ones in the bar, too.

'Meg?'

She looks up at the sound, aware she is hot and dusty.

Harry is standing in the doorway, his shirt back on but hanging loose over his breeches.

'I'm going to look for wood. Will you come?'

She looks down at herself and then her hands.

Harry laughs.

'We're going to collect wood. Not to the Squire's house.'

Jip barks enthusiastically and jumps up at Harry.

'Come on. Jip is keen.'

They walk on the path that Meg stumbled back along in the dark the previous evening. Bees are buzzing round clumps of pink sea thrift that has exploded into bloom in the sunshine. Swallows dip and weave over the marshy fields behind the path, while gulls arc and call to each other out at water.

Harry leads the way down on to the beach and Jip immediately picks up a stick to be thrown.

Harry obliges and tosses it way along the beach. Jip sets off in a shower of sand.

'Along there,' Meg points at some planks of wood thrown up beyond the tide line.

Harry nods and lopes towards them.

'Yes,' he says. 'These should do.' He brushes some sand off them and piles them up. 'Let's see if there are more.'

Meg takes off her stockings and boots and squishes the sand between her toes. She's forgotten how cleansing it is.

Harry turns and sees her. He grins and sits to take off his own boots. He dumps them with the wood and runs down to the sea. Jip bounds after him, splashing in the shallows.

Meg watches but then carries on, scanning the tide line for useful pieces of wood.

She feels Harry's footsteps thudding on the sand behind her.

'Hey, you don't want to paddle?' He touches her arm, and it almost scalds her.

'I'm looking for wood. I'd like the shutters mended.'

'They will be. I promise.' Harry's voice

is rich and earnest. ''Tis the least I can do after all the kindness you've shown us.'

'Let's get it back to The Anchor then,' Meg says. She's promised herself she won't let her guard down again, and she won't.

'Surely.' Harry nods. 'But a quick paddle first!'

He rushes at her and half pushes and half pulls her towards the water.

Meg isn't sure whether to laugh or to be angry. She tries digging her toes in the sand but there is no grip and Harry has her almost at the water's edge.

'My, you are a stubborn woman,' he says, flicking the hair back from her face which has come down from where she's tied it.

'Maybe I'd prefer not to get wet,' Meg says, slipping from his arms and starting up the beach again.

'Oh, no! You don't get away that easily!'

Harry starts after her and gathers her up in his arms. In two quick strides

Harry is knee deep in the water and he drops Meg down beside him. Jip dances beside him, barking.

But Jip's attention isn't on Meg or Harry any more. He puts his head under the water and begins rooting about.

Meg looks down as what he's doing and a chill runs through her, freezing her to the spot.

The body of a man, with a large dark stain across his caved-in chest, is floating gently, just under the water. The face is distorted and swollen and as pale as milk while thin hair waves like tendrils from his head.

16

'Ted Lancaster,' Harry says grimly. 'Shot by the excise men last evening.'

Meg splashes out of the water and up on to the beach. She stands shaking with one hand crushed against her mouth.

'Come away, Jip,' she calls, as her dog snuffles round the body.

Harry steps deeper into the water and hauls the dead man out by his jacket, dragging him up the sand almost to the tide line.

'We need to get him back to his wife and family before the excise men find him,' he says.

'Did you know he was here?' Meg asks, her voice low and breaking.

Harry turns to her and pinches the bridge of his nose.

'We rather hoped he'd be washed out to sea,' he says. 'The excise men turned up just as we were finishing, and your Pa and I and Ted rushed for the boat. Ted was hit and fell overboard. We couldn't find him in the water, and we couldn't stop to look, we had to row for our lives.'

Meg shivers.

Pa and Harry came within inches of being shot and she'd heard the muskets fire.

'What will his family do?' Meg asks. Her voice trembles and she can't stop shaking.

'Josiah will sort them, at least for now,' Harry says grimly. ''Tis worth his while so the excise men don't come snooping round. Will you go and get your father? We need to hide him until we can get a cart to collect him.'

Meg stumbles back to the Brewhouse.

Pa is explaining to Nat the process of making ale. The fire is going, and he is stirring the grains.

'Pa?' she calls gently. She doesn't want to frighten Nat. 'Pa? Out here a moment.'

Pa comes out of the Brewhouse, dabbing his forehead with a handkerchief. His face is red, and his forehead beading sweat but his jovial expression changes when he sees Meg.

'What is it, Meg?' he asks, a frown crossing his face.

'Ted Lancaster,' Meg says. 'We found his body —'

Her own body convulses, and she runs to the bushes to be sick.

'Oh, love,' Pa says pulling her close for a hug.

Meg wipes her mouth with the back of her hand.

'Harry says will you help him hide the body until he can get a cart from the village?'

'Yes,' Pa says. 'Young Nat is in there. Best you stay with him. He can't move himself.' And with that he heads off along the shore path in the direction Meg is pointing.

Meg tries to compose herself before she goes into the Brewhouse, but she is still shaking. Nat is sitting on a pile of sacks, idly twisting straws together in his hands.

Meg smiles at him.

'How are you feeling?' she asks, trying

to keep her voice light.

He looks up at her. His face is the same shape as Harry's, she notices, but his eyes and hair are darker. Still, there is no doubt in her mind they are brothers.

'Tired,' he admits.

'Do you want to come in the kitchen, or shall we try and get you back up to the attic?'

'Kitchen,' Nat says.

Meg goes over to him and offers her arm for him to lean on. She takes as much of his weight as she can, but he is very slow hopping to the kitchen. Whenever he puts his bad leg down, to steady himself or rest, he winces. And when he sits, he is sweating profusely.

'As soon as Harry is back, we'll get you upstairs again. Maybe today was too much.'

'No! It was nice. It was good to see something,' Nat says, but he sinks down on a stool in the kitchen and puts his head on his arms on the table and as Meg cuts onions and carrots for the pot, she can hear rhythmic breathing telling her he is asleep.

It is a long time until Pa and Harry are back. Harry's shirt is streaked and dirty. Meg tries not to think about what might be staining it.

'We returned him to his family,' Pa says, his voice soft.

'Children?' Meg asks.

Pa nods.

'Two boys and two girls.'

'What will become of them? How can this be worth it?'

'Josiah will make them a payment,' Pa says. 'Enough for a while, at least.'

Meg turns away to hide her frustration. Money might help for a while, but it won't keep them for ever if the breadwinner is gone.

She knows plenty of other jobs have a risk. Lord knows, enough fishermen go missing in these waters, but . . . she grinds one fist into the palm of her other hand.

'I'm out to the Brewhouse,' Pa says. 'Best get the lad upstairs.' He nods at Nat who is still asleep at the table.

'Can you manage?' Meg asks.

Harry nods but Meg and Jip follow him to the stairs and up to the bottom of the ladder.

'Best I put him over my shoulder,' Harry says, swinging Nat round like a sack of grain.

Meg cocks her head.

'Horses,' she hisses to Harry. 'Get Nat settled and pull the ladder up. It's William Rufus, I warrant.'

She hurries downstairs and slips out to the Brewhouse to warn Pa. They both take a quick look round. Everything seems in order.

William Rufus swaggers into the yard seconds later.

'Where's your help?' he asks looking around.

'Finding wood on the beach to fix the shutters.' The lie comes quickly to Meg.

William snorts.

'The place could do with tidying up.' His voice has an oily, patronising tone that makes Meg's toes curl. 'I hear Ted Lancaster died in the night,' he adds as

Meg struggles to keep her face straight. 'Fever, I was told.'

William looks hard at Pa as he says it.

'Shame,' Pa says, looking up and meeting his eye. 'One of my best customers.'

William rolls his eyes and glances round.

The Alehouse is quiet, and he must decide there is nothing for him because he spins round on his heel, takes his horse and mounts.

Meg waits for him to disappear along the shore path before she goes inside and calls for Harry.

'Nat's asleep,' Harry says. 'All the moving around must have exhausted him. What did that man want?'

'Investigating,' Meg says. 'He knew Ted Lancaster is dead.'

Harry pulls a face.

'That was quick. No secrets around here,' he mutters.

'He wanted to know where you were,' Meg says. 'I said you were out getting wood.'

'Wood!'

Harry bangs his fist against his forehead.

'Let's go and look then.'

They walk back out along the shore path. The tide is further in and thankfully Meg can no longer see where Ted's body was dragged from the water.

They find the wooden planks they first noticed earlier and pile them up to collect as they return.

'Look, there's more over there,' Meg points.

Soon they have a pile.

'There should be enough to fix all the shutters,' Harry says.

'Shall I get the wheelbarrow?' Meg asks.

Harry shakes his head.

'I can carry it.'

Meg shrugs but she bends down to grab a first plank just a Harry bends to take the same one. Their fingers meet on the dry wood and Meg feels a jolt through her body.

Harry's face is inches from hers and he stares into her eyes. She sees the grey of sea in his, turbulent, but warm and life giving.

Harry lets go the wood and weaves his fingers into her hair. Meg is aware of her heart drumming and blood rushing round her body as Harry pulls her face gently closer to his, bringing his lips down on hers.

She can taste salt on him as he presses closer to her. She looks up into his face and returns his kiss. Her hands grip his arms, and she hears him groan gently.

This is what it feels like to be with the right person, she thinks. This is what Ma and Pa had and she wouldn't find with William Rufus.

She is bursting with life and joy. Her skin tingles and she is weightless. She never wants this moment to end.

'I want to stay here with you for ever,' Harry says and Meg's heart skips to hear him say he feels the same way. 'But I fear we should take the wood home.'

They take the wood to the yard and as they stack it up Pa comes out of the Brewhouse.

'I had word,' he says to Harry with a meaningful look. 'We have to go fishing tomorrow.'

Meg glances from one of them to the other. She heard the words but feels certain Pa has another meaning entirely.

17

''Tis early for the salmon,' Meg says with a frown. 'The excise men may notice.'

Each year, in autumn, salmon and a lesser number of sea trout use the estuary as a route inland to the shallow rivers. The females wriggle a depression in sediments at the bottom of the streams and lay their eggs, which the male salmon come along and fertilise. The females are then so exhausted they die, so they must be caught on their way up stream on a rising tide.

'Let them,' Pa says. 'Chances are the first of the fish are arriving. They'll only see the nets and with luck a catch of salmon and trout.'

'Nothing else?' Meg asks, folding her arms across her chest, her voice flat.

'Nothing, however closely they watch,' Pa assures her, but Meg sees a glance flash between him and Harry.

The following morning Pa shows

Harry the traditional nets.

'We stand mid-stream, as many people as possible across the river,' he says. 'Each has a 'leg' in the centre to rest on the bed of the river. As the current gets stronger it gets harder to hold them but with luck you've got a full net by then.'

Together they check all the knots and there are no holes for the salmon to escape.

Two neighbours join them, bringing along their own nets, and Tom Larsen and his son have their boat out in the estuary. When the tide turns and is incoming and the men walk their nets out and form a line across the river, standing the longer middle leg into the mud of the estuary and tipping the net up to allow the incoming tide to fill them.

Meg hovers inside the public room, watching through the window. Pa is in the middle with one of the neighbours and Harry is furthest from her. She feels a slight flutter of worry that makes her stomach churn, but Harry is the tallest man out there, and Pa has been doing this every year and no harm has fallen him.

The sky is a dull silvery grey and the wind is picking up, adding a slight swell to the water, making little wavelets that break against the men. Their boots and stockings are piled in a heap on the shore as they've gone out barefoot, and already the water is inching past their knees.

Meg wonders if she should put on a stew for dinner. On fishing days, she can usually rely on a good catch to feed their patrons but the longer she watches the more convinced she is that it is not salmon that Pa is after.

Normally the fishermen would stand still midstream, but today they edge forwards and shuffle from side to side as if they are searching for more than fish.

Meg frowns. She can't see properly from inside. She goes out through the back, and she and Jip climb up on to the dyke in front of the Alehouse.

She sees Pa wave at Tom, who rows the boat closer. They both scan the shore before Pa pulls up a bundle wrapped in netting and weighted with rocks from the sea floor.

Harry strides over and takes Pa's net as Pa and Tom struggle to get the netting into the boat. Meg squints at them and leans forward to see better.

For a split second her breathing is suspended as her eyebrows rise. She understands what they have done. Wrapped up in the netting are half a dozen small barrels, probably gin or brandy. These must be the barrels from the other night that were taken away in the rowing boat under the noses of the excise men.

She exhales quietly. So they hid the contraband in the estuary this time. Always different places. Always one step ahead of the excise men.

Meg watches as the tide creeps in further and the muddy shoreline gets narrower. A heron, its long neck folded in flight, lands quite close to Meg and begins striding about, stopping to investigate something, and then moving on.

The men work the same way. They

step forward as a line, obviously feeling with their legs and feet for more nets. She hears a whistle and watches Tom as he manoeuvres the boat towards Harry and more barrels are loaded.

In half an hour the water has reached the fishermen's chests, and Meg is squeezing her fists. They should come in. It's too deep now to work and the tide will be strong. They are in danger of being dragged up stream with the fish.

She is about to call out when she hears the sound of hooves.

For a moment she wonders if Pa and Harry have heard, too, but they must have seen the approaching excise men because they have a quick conversation with Tom who then rows away from them towards the village. A quick glance at the boat appears to show a pile of fishing nets in the bow. The nets, as well as keeping the barrels together underwater, provide a good camouflage.

Meg keeps her eyes on the fishermen and does not look round at William Rufus even though she hears his horse whinny as it halts behind her and William's feet thud as he dismounts.

'Good fishing?' he asks, his voice sounding arrogant to Meg's ear.

She crosses her arms, turns, and gives him a fake smile.

'They gave Tom Larsen some,' she says as sweetly as she can manage. 'He's away to sell them in the village. We'll have to see what else they bring ashore. They should be coming in. The tide is rising.'

Sure enough Harry has moved over to Pa, and they are both dragging their nets towards the shore.

'Have you got many?' she shouts to Pa.

'Enough.'

His voice is thin across the water, but Meg nods and rushes back to the kitchen for a basket, leaving William and his two lackeys standing on the dyke watching.

'Good afternoon, William,' Pa is saying as Meg returns, hurrying down the shore with the big rush basket. The woven rim is fraying, and the twisted rush handles are worn but it's large enough to hold a good catch.

Pa takes a deep breath and swings his net out of the water.

It's not a huge haul, but enough, Meg hopes, to convince the excise men that this was a genuine afternoon's fishing.

The big fish gasp and gape in the air, and Meg swiftly grabs them from the net and drops them in the basket. Pa puts his net down with some relief and Harry pulls his net out of the water. Behind them, the neighbours are out of the water, too, and gathering their catch.

They don't look particularly pleased to see the excise men, but they have nothing but the fish and their nets. They collect their boots from the shore and with a wave to Pa and Harry make off along the dyke.

Harry's net has fewer fish than Pa, which doesn't surprise Meg. No doubt he didn't hold it steady or was too busy with their other mission.

'Good enough, eh?' Pa says.

William looks on, the scar pulling

down the side of his mouth.

Harry and Pa take one side of the basket each, pick up the nets and with a nod to William and their neighbours they start off towards The Anchor.

'There'll be salmon for dinner tonight if you're calling in,' Meg calls to William as she makes to follow them. Tonight, she can griddle the salmon for the customers and tomorrow will make a rich fish stew with the heads and tails.

Meg relaxes and looks out over the estuary. It is quiet with the rising tide. A few seagulls bob on the water but the salmon are too big for them. It is peaceful, but as much as she'd like to stay watching, she has a basket of fish to clean and gut ready for dinner, so she turns, whistles for Jip, and makes her way into the Ale house.

18

When Meg gets into the kitchen, she finds Pa sitting by the fire, his feet stretched out towards the grate while the flames crackle from the extra wood Pa has piled on and smoke twirls skywards.

'Get yourselves dry,' she says. 'That river must have been cold.'

'Right you are, lass,' Pa says. 'I am chilled through.'

Meg glances at him. It's unlike him to sit down and usually he'd argue he has something to do. She notices his cheeks have lost their ruddy appearance.

'I'll fetch some broth,' she tells him. 'And a dry shirt.'

She ladles broth from the stew pot that always hangs above the fire into a bowl, as a little niggle of worry worms its way into her thoughts. She remembers Mistress Cooper's warning to take care of her Pa. She frowns.

It might be summer, but the water

will have been unpleasantly cold, and Pa isn't getting any younger. Perhaps they shouldn't have taken the nets out. Surely they could have found the contraband with a boat.

'Needed to go out,' Pa says, as if hearing her thoughts. 'Never have found the stuff with the boat. Too much sediment churned up by the incoming tide.'

When Meg returns with a dry shirt, Pa has his clay pipe going and the air is smoky.

Harry has come inside and sits next to him, his long legs stretching towards the fire, too, but his cheeks are glowing from the outdoor activity. Pa sits hunched up as close to the fire as he can get as if his very bones are freezing.

'Away to your bed,' Meg tells him. 'Take my blanket, too, and get yourself warm. I can manage here.'

'I can help,' Harry says. 'It's the least I can do. Let me check on Nat and then I'll be back.'

Meg smiles and nods. For a moment she thinks her father will argue, but he doesn't and allows himself to be packed off to his bed, something Meg does not take as a good sign.

Harry is as good as his word. He helps Meg as she slices the fish down the belly and guts them. Heads and tails go in a pot ready for a fish stew.

She explains to him where the ale is and prices. As they stand in the Brewhouse, she notices the barrel of brandy and decides to take Pa up a nip.

He is asleep.

The Anchor is busy. It is the sort of evening in the Alehouse that Pa enjoys — being the host and rushing round talking to everyone comes naturally to him.

She watches Harry as she goes back and forth from the kitchen. He is a little stiff with customers, but he obviously knows some of the men and can chat with them about fishing, farming, and local life. If the drinks are not served as quickly as usual no-one appears to mind.

Meg cooks the salmon. It fizzes and splutters on the iron griddle before she dishes it up and adds a hunk of bread to the platters. If people ask, she says that Pa has taken to his bed and Harry is a relative come to help for a while.

Dusk is leaching the colour from the outside world, making both sky and sea a uniform grey when Meg hears the sound of horses' hooves outside and knows who their next guest will be. The room goes quiet as William Rufus strides in.

If he can feel the nervous, hostile atmosphere, the excise man chooses to ignore it. Instead, he peers around, his hand on his belt, as if monitoring all those inside. Meg feels the ripples of dislike aimed at him like tiny daggers.

He sits himself down in a corner and clicks his fingers at her.

'Where's your father?' he asks.

'Happen he's taken a fever,' Meg says. 'The water was cold, but we have plenty of fish. Harry is helping. Is it ale you're wanting? Dinner?'

William nods.

Meg keeps an eye on him as she turns a fish on the griddle. She can see William scowl as Harry puts down a tankard on the table for him.

But she is more worried about her father than she is about William. She takes a moment as the fish cooks to slip upstairs to check on him. He is wrapped in his blanket shivering.

'I can't get warm, Meggie,' he says. 'My bones are icy.'

'Oh, Pa,' Meg says, taking his hand in hers. The back of it is marked with liver spots that she hadn't noticed before, and all over his hands are white and red scars that he's got at different times from using knives and hammers, from brewing and from the fires. 'I'll fetch my cloak to put over you, too.'

Back in the public room, she scoops the fish off the griddle and piles it on to a platter for William.

'Fresh,' she tells him as he pokes at it. 'And well cooked.'

Not for the first time Meg thinks how nice it would be to have someone to cook for her. If she accepted William's offer of marriage then Pa could stay with them and find easier work, to say nothing of a house without draughts.

A guffaw from the other side of the room jolts her from that thought. Harry is laughing with some of the regulars. Meg sees a grimace cross William's face and she knows which of the two men she'd prefer, despite the fine townhouse and pretty frocks William's salary could buy.

It would be perfect if Harry were to stay here and run the pub, too. Meg watches him as he serves the regulars, allowing them to rib him about his service, and joining in with the banter. Another man about the place would relieve some of the pressure on Pa —

Pa!

There is still some of the willow juice that she had got from Mistress Cooper. That might bring Pa's fever down. It worked for Nat.

She rushes out of the public room to the kitchen, where Jip looks up with interest at her hurry. She pours water from the kettle into a tankard and adds a piece of bark from the packet on the shelf. Jip sniffs at the tankard and pulls back.

'Ah! Honey! Good thinking, Jip.'

Meg adds a spoonful of honey and carries the drink upstairs.

She makes Pa take a few sips before she will leave him. He pulls a face at the bitter liquid, and she gives a wry smile. It must be good for him if he doesn't like it.

When she gets back to the bar William Rufus has gone.

Harry comes up to her, putting a hand on her shoulder.

'How is your father?' he asks.

Meg shakes her head.

'Not good. I've given him some of the mixture I got for Nat.'

Harry nods and squeezes her shoulder before turning back to the customers. His presence is reassuring, and his touch confirms to her that they have something. Maybe he will stay. That would be a most comforting proposition.

She smiles at Harry, and he gives a

broad smile back that crinkles his eyes and dimples his cheeks just as another man, someone she doesn't recognise, in a leather jerkin, leather boots and a thick calico shirt enters the bar.

People turn with interest but none of the hostility that was directed at William Rufus is shown. The man rests his tricorne hat on the table and Harry rushes across to serve him. Several of the regulars gather round, too.

Meg cocks her head towards Harry but all he does is give her a slight shake of his head and Meg must work the rest of the evening watching and wondering.

It is not until the last of the customers has left, to weave an unsteady path along the dyke to their lodgings that Harry will speak to her.

As they collect the tankards and platters, damp down the fire, douse the lamps, close the shutters, and straighten the bar Harry tells her the man brought a message from Josiah.

'There will be another run tomorrow night,' he tells her as they step outside the kitchen door. 'Everyone is needed.'

The sky is now dark, with a milky band of stars splitting it almost in two. Occasional birds call out in the dark and insects chitter, while The Anchor creaks as it settles down for the night.

'That's not Josiah?' Meg asks.

Harry shakes his head.

'Just the messenger. I don't know who Josiah speaks to, but the word filters out like water running downhill.'

Meg turned to him with a gasp.

'But Pa?' she says. 'He's sick. He won't be able to go. It could kill him. It's not a risk I'm prepared to take.'

She looks up at Harry. She can't really see his face, but she feels his body tense.

'Aye, and Nat can't help either. Josiah must be short of men, especially if he sent word over here especially. He's not a man to cross.' Harry rubs a hand across his forehead.

'Don't want him accusing your Pa of working for a rival gang. Turn him against you and he's as dangerous as the excise men.'

Meg swallows.

'We'll have to see how Pa is in the morning,' she says but as she turns to go upstairs, she feels a great weight in her chest. She is sure Pa will be too unwell to work. In all her years she never remembers him taking to his bed before.

19

In the morning, as she feared, when Meg goes to check, she finds Pa burning up with a fever. She makes sure he is warm and insists he sips some of Mistress Cooper's mixture, but he is delirious and nothing he says makes sense. When he calls her Marie, her ma's name, it brings tears to Meg's eyes.

Harry finds her in the kitchen, stoking the fires and putting on the gruel for breakfast.

'He can't go out this evening,' she tells him. 'He's not just ill, he's making no sense.'

Harry knits his brows and rubs a hand over his face.

'He needs a bit of time. 'Tis a chill. Maybe this afternoon?'

Meg shakes her head. She is trying not to think about what might happen if he doesn't improve.

'No, he thinks I'm Ma. He doesn't

recognise me.'

She swallows and can't prevent a tear rolling down her face.

Harry steps over and pulls her close, rubbing her back. She falls into him, appreciating the comfort and contact.

'I'm sure he'll be fine,' he says. 'Look at Nat. He recovered from a musket ball. Your care and Mistress Cooper's potions —'

He lets the words hang in the air, but Meg isn't really thinking about Nat. She's wondering what she would do if Pa didn't get better. Her shoulders are tight, and she licks her lips.

They stand, locked together in the kitchen until Jip decides enough is enough and jumps up to be petted too. Meg breaks away with a jerky laugh and wipes her eyes with the back of her hand.

'I can't think of anyone to help,' Harry says. 'Most are either already tied to one gang or another or they're too old or dead against the work.'

Meg nods. But that thought sends her down another path. She spins around to

Harry and narrows her eyes.

'I'll do it,' she says, her face lighting up. 'I can carry the smaller barrels. I do it all the time here. I'll put my hair up and wear Pa's clothes. Just for tonight. Till he's better.'

Harry stares at her, his mouth agape. Then he rubs his chin, his hand rasping over his stubble.

'Never been a girl in the gang,' he says slowly. ''Tis hard and dangerous work.'

'But what choice is there if Pa can't go?'

Harry looks thoughtful.

'It might work. If we keep you at the back out of sight. You'll have to pull your weight, mind. It's not easy.'

'I know that,' Meg says. 'I'm not a fool.'

She doesn't add she saw them unloading the other night.

As Meg goes about her tasks for the day, she thinks about the night ahead. Working with the gang might give her a chance to see who is in charge if the mysterious Josiah makes an appearance.

176

If she can find out who he is, she can report him to William and stop this business . . .

It is only when Meg has added salt twice to the stew she chides herself. She must concentrate on the task at hand and stop daydreaming. She has no doubt it will be hard and dangerous. If the excise men find them, they could be arrested or shot, as Nat was.

She tries to carry on with her day as normal. She checks on Pa and Harry brings Nat downstairs so he can try walking again and get some fresh air. She is pleased he is looking better with each day.

As the day turns into evening, customers begin to arrive and Meg has a fish stew to serve. She is very aware of Harry moving round in the bar, easier this evening that the previous night, but The Anchor is not so busy, many of the regulars saving themselves for the night business.

When the final customers leave, Meg dresses in her father's clothes. His boots are too big, and she stuffs a stocking in the toe of each. She twists her hair up and piles it under Pa's big floppy hat and shows Harry her effort.

He frowns.

'' Twill be dark,' Meg says. 'And surely I'm the same size as Nat?'

'Hope it's well dark,' Harry says glumly.

'No-one will know me.'

'Don't speak,' Harry warns her.

Before they leave the public house Meg takes Jip upstairs to stay with her father.

It is almost dark, the sliver of moon tucked behind a cloud, leaving a silvery rim that reflects on the water, and a few stars glitter but are quickly swallowed up by the clouds.

'Good night for it,' Harry says with a nod.

They round the corner away from the river and walk a little further to where the dunes start, along the shore. Tonight, Meg is aware there are men hiding in dips in the sand, lying outstretched so as not to be seen. Harry and Meg join them, finding their own shallows to duck into.

They wait. Meg has an empty feeling in her stomach and is acutely aware of the sounds around her. It feels like hours, and she is struggling with the sand that has seeped into her clothing when they hear a repeated r-r-r-r sound, like a nightjar calling, close by.

Harry rests an arm on hers.

'The signal,' he whispers and pokes his head above the dunes. Meg wriggles forward and looks over the lip of their hollow. There is a light, out at sea, flashing on and off. From in front of them, in the dunes, an answering lantern is alternatively covered and uncovered.

'The boat is on its way.'

Harry's voice is so low Meg can barely hear it. Her heart hammers as they wait, but at last they hear the rhythmic creaking of oars and a faint splash as they dip into the water. This time, rather than a cutter being brought to the shore, the contraband has been loaded on to a smaller boat for landing.

Slowly and stealthily black shapes rise out of the dunes and almost a dozen men descend on the approaching boat. One holds it steady and Harry positions himself so he can help haul the barrels out giving them to the men to carry away up into the dunes.

Meg queues with the others, her feet in the shallow water. Harry gives her one of the smaller casks, but it is still heavy, and she feels the strain on her shoulders as she plods up the beach following the other men.

The rowing boat returns twice more with further booty. Each time Meg takes her place in the line and carries a barrel up to the dunes. Then the rowing boat vanishes and is replaced by a barge, low in the water, and they carry the barrels back down to fill it.

All the while, stationed in the dunes, lookouts watch for the excise men, but they are nowhere in sight.

Just as Meg thinks her arms will not lift another barrel, the barge takes off, half rowed and half punted along the coast towards the river estuary. It is quickly consumed by the darkness, but Meg knows it will make its way up stream for unloading and distribution to inland customers.

Men slink away into the night and Meg flops down on the beach. Her back is damp with sweat that is now chilling in the night air. Her arms ache and her shoulders are tense. But inside she is fizzing with excitement. They got away with it. Pa will be paid for the night's work, and no one will be any the wiser.

Meg and Harry don't speak as they walk home. With each step Meg's shoulders ache more and her feet drag. By the time they reach The Anchor the adrenaline has worn off leaving her exhausted with aching arms and her body racked with sudden shivers.

They get as far as the yard and Meg cannot walk any further. Her teeth are chattering and her body shaking. Harry's arms are round her as she sobs into his chest.

'It's fine,' he murmurs. 'You held your own. There are not many that could have done that. Josiah won't know and your father's place is secure.'

He helps her to the door and pushes it open so she can get inside. She checks her father and offers him Mistress Cooper's potion.

'Thank you, Meggie.' His voice is rusty and his chest rattles as he breathes. He has one hand stretched across Jip.

Meg lowers her aching body on to her own pallet. Pa has her blanket, so she pulls his oilskin over herself. She wonders if she should go to Mistress Cooper again and ask for a tonic for Pa, but before she can make a plan sleep overtakes her.

20

Meg wakes feeling fuzzy and tired. She immediately knows something is wrong. There is a different feel to the air.

Then she hears wood being sawn and pieces dropping on top of each other with a hollow clunk. Someone is already up and working.

She looks across at the window and realises the problem. It is far later than she normally wakes. She can feel the warmth of the sun against the shutters, and the light that penetrates the many cracks is bright and golden.

The sounds are different, too. No dawn chorus as the world coughs its way into life. The water birds are squabbling for food, and somebody is whistling in the distance.

Still hovering on the edge of sleep, Meg listens for her father filling the barrels or singing tunelessly as he stokes a fire to heat the hops and barley. But it is not her father who has woken her. It is someone else she can hear.

Meg frowns and half rises. In shock, she realises she is still wearing her father's shirt, jerkin and breeches. She was so tired last night she didn't even undress. His oilskin is crumpled beneath her, too.

Now as she tries to move, her shoulders scream out in pain and her arms are heavy. She half walks and half drags herself to the window and pushes the shutters open.

It must be mid-morning already. She's never slept so late.

She looks down at her clothing and grimaces. She should find her dress and return these to her father's room.

Pa!

She rolls her shoulders to try and get her muscles working, then collects Pa's clothes and tiptoes across to his room. He is no better, but no worse. His breathing is raspy, and he coughs and mutters in his sleep.

She lays a hand on his forehead and

frowns. It is difficult to tell if he is fever-ish, but he's had a turbulent night. The blankets are twisted around him. She straightens things out as best she can and goes to check on Nat.

The boy is sitting on his pallet twist-ing a bit of straw in his hands, a smile on his face.

'How are you?' Meg whispers although she hardly need ask the question.

'Can I come down?' Nat asks. 'There is nothing to do here.'

'Let me check downstairs first,' Meg says. 'I'll get you some gruel and ask Harry.'

Nat beams at her and Meg immedi-ately feels better. Both the brothers are nice people.

Meg slowly makes her way downstairs, the pain smarting in her arms, shoulders and back. The kitchen door is open, and the fire has already been stoked. She smiles gratefully and puts a pan with water and oats on to cook.

When she goes to the yard Harry is bent over, sawing the planks of wood they collected. He already has a pile the right lengths for new shutters.

'Don't you sleep?' she asks.

'Your Pa woke me with his coughing,' Harry said. 'Thought I'd make a start on repairing The Anchor.'

Meg nods and turns to go inside.

'Feeling all right?' Harry catches her arm before she disappears.

Meg can't help but wince.

'A bit stiff,' she admits.

''Twill wear off,' Harry says with a grin. 'Might take a couple of days, though.'

Meg scowls.

'Nat wants to come down.'

'He can help me with this,' Harry says, gesturing at the wood. 'Maybe his leg will take his weight. I'll fetch him down in a bit, shall I?'

Meg nods.

'I'm preparing breakfast,' she says.

She goes back into the kitchen and fetches honey and bowls and spoons for the table. She leans her head against the fireplace as she reaches to stir the porridge.

A sudden thought makes her freeze.

She didn't notice if Josiah was there last night. She didn't notice anyone in charge of it all. She had been so busy keeping her head down and playing her part she'd forgotten one of the main reasons for going.

She could understand now why batsmen were posted because there was no way that those who were unloading from the boats could keep an eye out for the revenue men.

She scolds herself mentally and eases herself upright when she hears voices outside in the yard.

Meg turns and cocks her head on one side.

Harry is speaking in a whisper, but the other voice is a woman's, and not so quiet.

Meg tiptoes to the side of the kitchen door where she has an oblique line of sight to the yard.

Harry is leaning in the doorway of the Brewhouse, his back against one side and an arm stretched across to the other. In front of him is a woman, whom Meg can only see side on. She is tall, blonde, and well dressed, in a vibrant cornflower blue dress and crisp white apron. The dress has a lace collar and lace at the sleeve edges. She has topped it with a dark blue shawl against the late summer chill.

Meg has no doubt the woman has dressed to impress, and the thought doesn't cheer her up.

'I can't. Nat is still ill,' Harry is saying.

The woman stamps her foot and makes a dismissive gesture with her free hand.

Meg looks down at her clothing and grimaces. She should go back to the fire and stir the gruel but for the moment she is too intrigued watching the interaction between Harry and the woman.

Harry straightens up and wipes a hand over his brow.

The woman puts her hands on her hips and leans toward him. She says something that Meg doesn't hear but suspects might be an ultimatum.

Harry had kissed her the other day.

Did it mean nothing? Was he toying with her for the sake of the help she and Pa were giving Nat?

Thoughts spin and twist in her head but the main thing that concerns her is, how can she compete with this striking woman? She can't. She has no cornflower blue dress, and her hands are inlaid with grime and smell of fish. She blinks to keep tears from her eyes and watches as Harry wrinkles his nose and squeezes his eyes shut.

Meg swallows and tries to quell the knot in her stomach. Harry hasn't mentioned a woman, but he hasn't spoken much about where he comes from.

Before she can do anything, however, the drumbeat of a horse's hooves sounds from the embankment, and sure enough William Rufus steers his horse into the yard and dismounts.

No doubt he's heard about last night's business and has come to question them all, Meg thinks wryly.

Meg pulls back from the doorway. She doesn't want William, or Harry, for that matter, to see her.

'And who is this?' William doesn't keep his voice down and Meg notices it has taken on a syrupy edge. She can almost hear him salivating over the woman and to her horror she sees Harry stiffen and step closer.

Meg tells herself that whatever Harry wants to do is up to him. She has no ties to him but even as she thinks it, she can feel her heart twisting.

She doesn't hear if Harry replies but William's voice purrs.

'What a lot of relatives Archie Parton has,' he says.

Harry straightens up and Meg wills him not to argue with the excise man. It doesn't do to have him on the wrong side, and William won't take any rebuke well.

She sees the woman smile at William and his attention is diverted from Harry who leaves them talking and ducks into the Brewhouse.

21

Meg berates herself. She should never have allowed her heart to take over her head. Now she will look a fool and worse, she feels a fool.

At some point she is aware the voices outside have stopped but she refuses to go and see. She is spooning the gruel out into wooden bowls when Harry appears in the doorway, blocking out the light. His face is in shadow so Meg cannot see his expression.

'Will you take this up to Nat?' Meg asks. 'He's itching to be up. I'm going to see Pa.'

Harry nods.

He takes one bowl and climbs the stairs and Meg takes another and follows him. Questions splutter on the tip of her tongue but she swallows them back. Harry will tell her if he wants. It is his business. She presses her lips together.

Meg crouches down beside Pa.

'Pa?' she whispers.

'Mmmm.' His eyes are closed but she think she is aware she is there.

'I've brought you some breakfast. See if you can sit up and take a little.'

Pa tries to shake his head, but Meg is having none of it. She puts the bowl down and heaves him up, so his head is at least higher. She loads a spoon with the gruel and pushes it against his lips.

Pa resists at first but as Meg pushes, he gives in and accepts a spoonful. She continues spooning, a great deal dribbling down his chin, until he turns his whole head away, moaning gently.

'I'll leave you to get some sleep,' she tells him. 'I'll bring you some soup at lunchtime.'

By the time she gets back downstairs again Harry and Nat are outside, their bowls emptied and left on the table.

Harry is back sawing the planks and Nat sits on a pile of wood throwing a stick for Jip.

'Look, Meg,' Nat calls, and stands up,

putting most of his weight on his injured leg.

'Excellent,' Meg says. 'You'll soon be well enough to go home.'

Nat grins.

'I like it here,' he says. 'I like being by the sea.'

Meg looks around. She can see two ships out on the water. There is only a slight swell, but the wind is coming from the sea bringing the smell of salt and seaweed to The Anchor.

Sometimes, she thinks, she takes it all for granted and doesn't look out at what they have enough.

'It's fine today,' she agrees. 'But wait until winter settles in and the waves are trying to pound on the front door and the wind is pulling the thatch from the roof.'

Nat opens his eyes wider.

'Well, the shutters will all be good for this winter,' Harry chips in. 'Hopefully I can replace them all.'

Meg refuses to meet his eye.

'Grand,' she says and goes back into

the kitchen.

Meg is acutely aware of Harry and Nat outside all morning as she goes about her regular tasks. At noon she calls them in for some soup and bread but excuses herself and take a bowl up to Pa.

At some point during the afternoon, she goes out to the garden to get some vegetables. Jip follows her, scrabbling in the mud as if to help her before suddenly he stands stock still, then races out on to the dyke, barking madly.

'Meg!'

She looks up at the voice, wincing as her back unwinds.

'Eliza!'

She's pleased to see her friend and leans forward to kiss her cheek, keeping her dirty hands back.

'Come into the kitchen and I'll make some tea,' she says, dropping the carrots by the pump and washing her hands.

Eliza is caught by the activity in the yard and nods to Harry and Nat before following Meg into the dark kitchen.

'Who is that?' she demands as soon as

they are inside.

Meg blinks.

'Cousins,' she says flatly, sticking to the line they told William Rufus.

Eliza narrows her eyes.

'You don't have any cousins,' she says. 'Your ma's family all died, and your Pa's brother went to sea never to be seen again.'

'Cousins,' Meg says again and gives Eliza a pointed look.

'Oh,' Eliza says. 'That sort of cousin. Well, I wish you'd told me they were here. I'd have paid a visit before.' She grins broadly at Meg and for the second time today Meg feels out dressed and out classed by those visiting The Anchor.

'Well, happen they'll be away soon,' she says, giving Eliza a disapproving look. 'And we'll be back to normal. Well, here's hoping. Pa is ill with a fever.'

'Oh. I hope he recovers soon, Meg. But meanwhile you are lucky to have such help around the place.' She gives Meg a knowing look, which Meg refuses to acknowledge.

'Tell me, do you have any work for Squire Padgett's family at the moment?'

Eliza thins her lips.

'Not this again, Meg.'

'No, no. Tell me.'

Eliza sighs and drops her shoulders.

'Not at the moment,' she says. 'The Squire is away but his wife contacted Mama to say he has purchased a bolt of cloth for winter walking frocks, so as soon as we have word we'll be going there to work.'

Meg lets Eliza prattle on about what she is doing and where she's been. She murmurs assents occasionally, which seems to keep Eliza satisfied.

There is a crash of wood, and a splintering and splitting noise then a cry from Harry, followed by a shriek of laughter from Nat.

Eliza shoots Meg a wide-eyed look and they both jump up and hurry outside.

Harry is alternately shaking his hand and sucking his finger, whilst on the ground lies a shattered shutter.

'Harry dropped it,' Nat says gleefully.

'Are you all right?' Eliza asks, stepping forward. 'Let me see your hand.'

''Tis fine,' Harry growls, putting his hand behind his back.

'Let me see,' Eliza says again, and Harry slowly brings his hand forward.

His index finger has a big deep cut on it.

'Run it under the pump,' Eliza says. ''Twill take the sting from it. Meg, do you have a cloth to bandage it?'

Meg goes inside to find a cloth.

When she comes out Eliza is holding Harry's hand.

Meg offers Eliza the bandage, to which Eliza arches an eyebrow. She can't do it one handed.

Without looking at Harry, Meg ties the bandage.

'There,' Eliza says, smiling at both of them. 'You should be able to work now.'

'Thank you, ma'am,' Harry says.

'It's Eliza,' Eliza says with a giggle.

'Excuse me,' Harry says, gesturing the broken shutter. 'I want to replace this one before customers arrive.'

Soon after Eliza takes her leave, but not before she's given Meg the benefit of her advice.

'It's no good,' Meg tells her friend. 'He's spoken for.'

'That's not what I saw,' Eliza replies. 'I'd say he's out to impress you.'

'I don't think so. And besides they'll be gone soon. 'Tis but a brief cousin visit.'

Meg keeps out of Harry's way for the rest of the day feigning work in the kitchen and visits to Pa when he is about.

Before too many customers arrive, Harry takes Nat back up to the attic. Nat is delighted he can climb the stairs on his hands and knees. Meg realises that what she said is true. Nat is getting better. They won't need to stay much longer.

Harry remains quiet and thoughtful and doesn't speak to Meg, either. She isn't sure if he is embarrassed or angry at the woman's appearance this morning but they are dancing around each other, allowing the other plenty of space.

As customers begin drifting in for the evening Harry works stoically but doesn't laugh or joke with them.

She is in the kitchen when William Rufus returns but she sees him immediately, laying his hat on a table and stretching his legs out. Meg watches carefully as many customers keep their voices down and give him shifty looks while Harry goes to serve him.

'Where's that delightful relative of yours?' William asks. 'Sissie? Was that her name?'

She sees Harry's cheeks colour and notices his fists clench although he keeps them by his side out of sight of William.

'She left again,' he tells William.

'Ah, that's a shame. I was hoping to get to know her,' William says. Harry turns away but William calls after him.

'A tankard of your finest. None of that watered-down stuff mind.'

Meg is so busy serving meals and drinks she doesn't notice for a while that Harry has gone, leaving her to finish up and close The Anchor for the night.

She checks upstairs in the attic but there is only Nat curled up and asleep. There is no one in the bedrooms except Pa and the Brewhouse is empty. She stands at the front door and calls softly into the night, but Harry doesn't answer.

22

When Meg wakes in the morning her room is dark. She is puzzled. She can hear sounds from outside along the estuary and the heavy drumming of rain on the roof.

She sits up slowly, still aware of her painful shoulders, but the stiffness is not as acute as the previous day.

When she walks across to the window and pushes the shutters, she realises why it is dark. Harry has removed the old shutters with the fractured wood along the bottom and poorly matched seams. These new ones cover the window completely and effectively darken the room.

Meg lifts her chin and gives a small smile of satisfaction. This will make a huge difference to the room in winter. With any luck she'll no longer have to stuff the crevices and gaps with straw and cloth to keep out the icy winds.

For a moment she wonders how many

of the shutters he's managed to replace. Then she remembers the woman who turned up yesterday. Sissie, according to William Rufus, who was obviously quite smitten with her.

'Oh, well. Maybe she'll keep him away from here,' Meg mutters as she wrestles with her frock and petticoats. Her shoulders are still taut and she wriggles on the spot to loosen them.

Then a thought hits her like another stab of pain. Harry wasn't around last night. Did he come back?

She stares out at the estuary. Rain is beating down, churning up the water into a frothing mass. There is a chill to the air, reminding Meg that summer is nearly over. She wonders if Harry will really do the roof as he's promised.

If he's unreliable she'll have to nag Pa into doing something about it. The Anchor won't survive without some work before winter.

She quickly finishes dressing and climbs the ladder to the attic. Nat is awake and fiddling with bits of straw from the roof.

'If you keep pulling our straw out we'll have no roof for the winter,' Meg chides.

'Ha!' Nat points at several places where water is dripping through the thatch and pooling on the floor. 'Anyway, Harry is going to fix it for you.'

'Where is Harry?'

Nat shakes his head.

'He wasn't here when I woke up.'

Meg frowns. Was he out all night?

Then she shakes her head. He's a grown man and not beholden to her. If he wants to stop out all night, it's no business of hers.

She presses her lips together.

'Can I come down, Meg?'

Meg glances at the ladder.

'I can't carry you,' she warns.

'I can manage. I can use my knee.'

'I'll go first and try and catch you if you fall.'

Nat manages the ladder without too much difficulty. He really is well on the way to recovery.

'I must check on Pa,' Meg tells him.

'Can you manage the stairs?'

Her father is no better.

'Meggie,' he murmurs as she wipes his hair back from his brow.

'Here,' she says. 'Take another sip of Mistress Cooper's remedy.'

'Horse medicine,' Pa mutters, which Meg takes as a good sign. At least he's registering what she is giving him.

'I'll go and fetch some breakfast,' she tells him.

Nat has put some more logs on the kitchen fire and stoked it up. He has also opened the back door and is calling for Harry.

'Is he there?' Meg asks.

Nat shakes his head.

'Did he say anything to you?' she asks.

Nat shakes his head again.

'I thought he might be out here working already. He did two of the shutters yesterday even after he hurt his hand.'

Nat is jittery, checking behind the door and in the Brewhouse, even though it's clear to Meg that Harry is not here.

She makes them all some breakfast.

The hens have been laying well so she cooks eggs for herself and Nat and takes Pa up some gruel. Again, it is a challenge to make him eat. He is coughing badly.

It continues to rain all day. The air in the Alehouse is damp, despite Meg stoking up the fires. Nat is bored and her father's coughs echo round the place. Each time Meg glances out of the windows it is to see puddles and splashes. She can barely make out the estuary and doesn't see any ships for the rain.

The evening is slow with very few customers. Those that do come in shake themselves off like wet dogs and stand by the fire cradling drinks in their hands for a long time.

When Pa is no better in the morning, she makes the decision to go to see Mistress Cooper again. She has eggs she can exchange.

'I need to go to the village,' she tells Nat. 'I suggest you shut and lock the kitchen door. You can stay downstairs but don't go outside. You're still not able to move on that leg and there is always a chance the excise men will be round looking for someone with gunshot wounds.'

Nat pouts and for a moment Meg thinks he will argue with her.

'Stay with Nat, Jip,' she whispers to him, scratching the top of his head.

Nat at least looks mollified by the promise of a companion and Meg fetches her bonnet and cloak and a basket to carry the eggs in.

Outside the weather is still unwelcoming. The sky is the dirty grey colour of fire ashes, and a breeze has blown up making the estuary choppy with muddy wavelets.

Before long Meg feels the damp soaking into her skirts and as much as she tries to edge round the puddles on the path, she can't help but splatter mud and water up as she goes.

Meg pulls her cloak tighter around her shoulders and holds the hood in place as she hurries along the earthen path. Someone waves at her as she passes but Meg isn't sure who it is seen through the damp haze. Still, she gives a wave back.

As she draws closer to the village, Meg sees Squire Padgett's carriage bowling along the main street. She stops to watch it, wondering if the Squire is back yet, but it is his wife and daughters inside.

Yet again she is pondering the problem of who Josiah might be when she catches a glimpse of William Rufus in the distance.

She doesn't want another encounter with him. Rather than face him she turns sharply into the churchyard through the lych gate and takes the path up to the church porch.

She presses herself against the wall of the porch, hoping William will pass and she can come out and go about her business, but she hears his horse coming slowly along and sees his head over the hedge peering around.

She clenches her jaw until she can feel a stiffness in her neck. Why can't he go on past? Why does he need to seek her out?

Meg scans the graveyard. There is

nowhere to hide unless she wants to crouch behind a gravestone, so she takes the only other option available and opens the big wooden door of the church and slips inside.

It is cool in the church and there is a smell of candle wax and incense. Only a couple of the sconces are lit, and it is dim. She looks about to see if there is any sign of the Reverend Green, but the church appears empty.

She wanders towards the altar and looks up at the carved figure on the cross. The peaceful face of the poor man hanging there had intrigued her as a child and thinking about him had kept her occupied through many a long sermon.

Meg is about to turn and leave, when she hears footsteps in the side aisle to her right. She turns expecting to see the minister or a worshiper but there is a dreadful screech, like an animal's scream in the night, and then the footsteps stop.

Meg freezes and puts a hand to her chest. She swallows hard and then tiptoes along the pew towards the side aisle.

When she gets there, she can see what has made the noise. A wooden trapdoor in the floor has been lifted and folded back on to the church's paving stones. Meg blinks. She has never noticed this in all her years coming to church. She creeps forward until she can see what is below the floor.

A set of stone steps lead down into a dark area below. There is a dull light down there, that moves from side to side, making shadows reach and stretch across the steps. The air coming up is even cooler than in the church and has a fusty, earthy smell.

Suddenly the light is spun around so that Meg can see a lantern but not who is holding it. A candle glows from within.

For a moment Meg considers leaving the church quickly and pretending she wasn't there but in the low light she catches a glimpse of something, several things in fact, standing on the floor and made of wood. They look very much like the barrels she carried off the boat the other night.

Is this where the contraband is stored? Meg wonders. Is the Reverend Green involved in the night business or is someone using the church without his knowledge? She thinks about the small man, with his broken complexion and boring sermons. Surely he wouldn't be. It wouldn't sit well with his calling.

She is about to step down into the crypt when a voice from the far end of the church hails her.

Meg turns quickly, the smooth sole of her boot spinning on the stone floor of the church.

'Eliza!'

'Meg, what are you doing in here? Come, now. The river is rising. Word is it will flood again.'

23

Meg is hesitant despite Eliza's pleading. She should see who is down in the crypt and see if those were the barrels they had unloaded the other night. If she leaves, the contraband may be spirited away before she has another chance.

But Eliza is tugging at her arm.

'Meg, come on. The river is rising. Word is in the village it may come over the dyke.'

'What?' The tremor in Eliza's voice brings Meg back to the moment. 'Flood?'

Eliza nods furiously.

'But I've got to get to Mistress Cooper. I need something for Pa. He's not well.'

'You'd better go now,' Eliza says. 'Before it's too late for you to get back to The Anchor.'

The words spark fear in Meg. What will Pa and Nat do if she isn't there? Nat won't know how dangerous the water can be, and when she left, Pa was in no position to direct him.

She allows Eliza to pull her out of the church into the porch where they both pause to pull up the hoods on their cloaks. The rain is still coming down in sheets, making it hard to see across the churchyard.

Trees sway in the wind, and leaves are being ripped from the branches, falling on the ground to be pummelled into a wet green mass on to the path like limp, boiled cabbage.

Out on the road, water is already lying, and they have to splash through it to get to Mistress Cooper's cottage. Meg doesn't know if William Rufus is still around, but she doesn't stop to look.

When Mistress Cooper opens the door and gestures them in, Meg hurries to stand by the fire stepping on to a small reed mat in front of the grate. She shivers and takes a deep breath as she watches her cloak and dress gently steam.

'What can I do for you, Meg Parton?' Mistress Cooper says.

Meg sees Eliza gazing round the

main room of the cottage that Mistress Cooper uses as a workshop with the big table in the middle covered in bottles, jars, papers and herbs.

''Tis Pa,' she tells Mistress Cooper. 'He's taken a chill and can't seem to shift it. It's very unusual for him to take to his bed. I don't remember —' Her voice breaks and she has to pause and blink back tears before she can continue. 'I don't remember him so ill.'

Eliza takes a step towards her and puts her good arm about Meg. She has taken off her bonnet and her dark curls bounce round her face.

'I'm sure he'll be well soon.' Eliza rubs Meg's shoulder.

Mistress Cooper makes a dismissive sound in the back of her throat.

Meg stares at her, trying to deduce the meaning of the sound. Today Mistress Cooper is wearing a dress of dark green wool. Her apron is stained to match with many shades of green from teal through jade to Lincoln green. Meg notices Mistress Cooper's fingers are stained green, too, and several bowls and kitchen mortars on the table contain a green paste.

'I told you to take care of him,' Mistress Cooper's words break through Meg's thoughts.

'He went fishing,' Meg says miserably. 'I made him sit by the fire straight after and put him to bed. I've been giving him the willow bark tea you sent but it doesn't seem to help.'

'No,' Mistress Cooper says.

'What else can I try?' Meg asks.

Mistress Cooper moves to her table.

'Elderflower,' she says, reaching above her head and pulling down a spray of drying leaves and flowers. 'And catnip and yarrow. Let me make you a packet.'

Mistress Cooper turns away from them and busies herself at the table.

Eliza grips Meg's arm tighter and raises her eyebrows.

Meg smiles back at her friend. She knows Mistress Cooper alarms some people, but she'd trust her with her life.

While she waits, she peers out of the tiny cottage windows. Mistress Cooper has plants growing up the walls and close to the house and Meg can see the leaves are all heavy with water and dripping.

'Here,' Mistress Cooper holds out a small parcel to Meg. 'Make it into a tea, and I'll warrant he'll be well soon enough.'

'Thank you,' Meg says. She unloads the eggs she has brought on to the table and slips the package into her basket.

She glances at Eliza, who waves her bad arm and arches her eyebrows at Meg.

Meg gives a little shake of her head, but Eliza has already stepped forward towards Mistress Cooper.

'Mistress?' she asks. 'Can you do anything for my arm?'

Mistress Cooper gives her a long hard stare and Meg feels her face flush for her friend.

'Why would you change yourself?' Mistress Cooper asks. ''Tis something that is part of you. Not something that can be fixed.'

'But I hate it,' Eliza cries. 'Everybody

stares at me.'

'Tsssh,' Mistress Cooper scoffs. 'People may stare at you, but not for the arm.'

'Nobody notices,' Meg joins in, trying to comfort her friend.

'They do,' Eliza says. 'No man will look at me. They worry I won't be able to run a house or do what needs to be done. Or that a babe will be born the same way. Some people say I'm cursed, even.'

Meg gasps.

She hasn't heard Eliza complain like this before. She thought her friend had reconciled herself with her deformity. She certainly hasn't allowed it to hold her back with her work. She and her mother are held in high regard as seamstresses in the village.

'Ah, a man, is it?' Mistress Cooper asks. 'That is not the same.'

'What do you mean?' Eliza asks.

''Tis love that worries you, not the arm, I believe,' Mistress Cooper says. 'That is entirely a different problem.'

Meg glances at her friend.

'Can you do anything about it?' Eliza asks.

'There is no need to worry,' Mistress Cooper says. 'These things will right themselves.'

Meg sees Eliza gathering herself up to say something and jumps in first.

'And me?' she asks. 'How am I to be in love?'

Mistress Cooper regards them both for a moment.

'You are both young,' she says. 'There is no cause for worry or alarm. All will be well. There is nothing I can give you that will hurry the process. What will be will be.'

Eliza snorts, but Meg wonders what the healer means. She knows the woman is blessed, or cursed, with second sight. It would help if she would share what she saw more directly but still, if Mistress Cooper sees no problems in their futures, she for one is prepared to believe her.

She smiles.

'Thank you,' she says. 'And thank you

for the tea. I'll away home and give it to Pa now.'

Mistress Cooper turns and looks towards the door.

''Tis not the fever nor even love that is your problem,' she says. 'You have other problems to deal with at the moment.'

Meg swallows. She does, but she is no nearer finding out who Josiah is or releasing Pa from his grip.

She nods agreement and thanks to Mistress Cooper and grabs Eliza's arm and pulls her friend gently towards the door.

The healer opens it for them to step outside and the rain hurls itself at them, almost knocking Meg from her feet. The weather has definitely got worse while she's been in the cottage and the sky is now so dark it could almost be night-time. She can't help a shudder as the wind twists and nips at her clothing.

24

The street outside Mistress Cooper's cottage is now under water. Meg and Eliza do their best to sidestep deep puddles but all the same Meg can feel damp creeping into her boots.

She wonders idly if Harry could repair them but then remembers in a spike of anger that Harry has disappeared, leaving her with Nat, Pa sick and the waters rising.

She twists her plait round and pulls up the hood on her cloak.

Meg is about to head towards the river and the dyke to head home when she remembers the church. She draws Eliza across the road and to the path up to the church.

'Where are we going?' Eliza asks, still tugging on the hood of her cloak. 'I thought you needed to get straight back to see to your Pa.'

'I saw something in the church.' Meg

has to shout to be heard over the rainfall that drums on leaves, the path and themselves. She risks a look around but there is no one in sight.

'What?' Eliza asks. 'What could be more important than getting home?'

'I thought I saw some barrels in the crypt,' Meg says.

Eliza stops and Meg has to stop.

'Meg, when are you going to give this up?'

'I can't. It's killing Pa. He can't continue to be out all nights. He went fishing to look for the barrels they had to dump when the excise men were after them, and now he has a dreadful chill. If I don't put a stop to it, it will kill him.'

'Why don't you let Sergeant Rufus take care of it? Tell him if you think there are barrels in the church.'

'I will. I will. But I just want to check first. I don't want him to think I'm leading him on.'

Eliza looks at her.

'What?' Meg says.

'Are you?' Eliza asks, looking up at

Meg from under her eyelashes. 'Leading him on.'

'I don't mean that. I mean telling falsehoods about the smuggling. He'll never believe anything I say again if I give him false information.'

'Mightn't it be dangerous?' Eliza asks.

Meg shrugs.

'We'll be out of the rain in the church,' she says.

Meg leads the way through the churchyard and up to the porch where she pushes down her hood and shakes her head to clear the raindrops on her face.

Eliza follows her example before Meg opens the church door as quietly as she can.

She steps inside and puts a finger to her lips. They stand listening but Meg can hear nothing.

'There's no-one here,' Eliza whispers.

Meg nods and leads the way to the side aisle where she had seen the trap-door. There is barely enough light to see.

She walks along the aisle tapping with

her foot. When the sound changes to a hollow noise she knows she's found it. She bends down — the wooden door is difficult to make out. Given that few parishioners would ever come to this part of the church she is not surprised she's never noticed it before.

'Here,' she whispers to Eliza.

'What?' Eliza asks. 'I can't see anything.'

'Feel the ground,' Meg says, putting her basket on a pew and bending down. 'Here, feel the metal ring. It's flush with the wood.'

Eliza obediently bends and feels the latch.

'What's down there?' she asks.

'I saw something, connected to the night business, if I'm not mistaken.'

'But it's a crypt,' Eliza says. 'It'll be full of corpses and bones.' Her voice rises a notch.

'We don't have to go down there,' Meg says. 'I just want to open the door and have a look.'

She is aware of Eliza pulling back a

little and senses her friend's reluctance.

'Come on, Eliza. Just a look.'

She takes the metal ring in both hands and heaves at it.

She can't make it move.

She strains again, getting up from her knees and bending over it. She puffs out her cheeks.

'It's really heavy. Can you help?'

Eliza comes closer and puts her good hand on the ring.

'Urghhh. It's not moving.'

Eliza steps back and brushes her hand down.

'It must open. Come on, one more try.'

Eliza comes back and takes the ring again. Meg strains as hard as she can and feels the wooden door shift.

'Nearly,' she says.

Meg pulls again, grinding her teeth and panting with the effort. She can't help thinking there must be something down here if it is difficult to get in.

Just as she thinks she can't continue the door lifts and rises quite quickly. Meg steps forward and wedges her shoulder under it. The muscles in her back scream with pain.

The wood is heavy and together she and Eliza get under and heave so that it swings open and thumps back on to the stone slabs of the floor behind it, leaving a dark opening in front of them.

Meg jumps as the bang echoes round the church. Dust is disturbed, billowing up from the floor like clouds, and there is a flutter of wings as the sparrow moves from beam to beam.

Eliza clutches hold of her and looks around. Meg can feel blood pumping round her body. She is on edge, waiting. Someone must have heard the enormous noise, but no-one comes and slowly she manages to breathe deeply and force her heart to quieten down.

'Phew,' she breathes out slowly. 'That was difficult.'

The air from the opening is chilly and fusty.

'You're not going down there?' Eliza asks. There is a tremor in her voice.

'I've got to check,' Meg says.

'You won't be able to see. It's dark.'

Meg thinks for a moment.

There are a couple of sconces by the church door, giving a little light.

'Wait here. I'll get a candle,' Meg says.

She tries to ignore the look of alarm on Eliza's face as she dashes away down the aisle. The sconces are set high in the wall, and she can't reach up to get the candles.

She slaps her thigh in frustration and looks around. It's gloomy in the church but there must be some way that the Reverend Green lights these candles. He's not much taller than her.

Just as she is about to give up and go back to Eliza, Meg finds the stool. It has been pushed behind a column. She drags it across to the wall and grasps one of the candles, climbing down slowly and shielding the flickering light with her hand as she carries it back to Eliza.

'Here,' she says. 'Light.'

'I'm not going down there.'

Eliza shivers and Meg feels the chill

and damp from outside penetrating her own clothing. She doesn't want to go down, either, but the only way to protect Pa is to sort this out. Isn't that what Mistress Cooper said? And Harry told her himself that there was no way out for Pa as things stood.

She takes a deep breath.

'Wait for me,' she says. 'Don't go anywhere.'

Eliza gives a tight nod.

Meg bends down, the candle held up in one hand. She can see several steps leading down. Gingerly she puts one foot on the first step into the crypt and then the next. The steps are not wide, and she holds on to the trapdoor frame, so she doesn't fall.

After half a dozen steps, she can see into the crypt and can investigate under the church. The light is not good, but she immediately notices the walls rise to an arched roof.

Meg creeps further down the steps, the air getting chillier with an earthy odour. She holds the candle out in front of herself. The floor near the steps is clear of anything and her boots echo as she treads down on the big stone slabs.

She moves a couple of paces away from the steps and can immediately see things piled up against the walls.

'What can you see?'

Eliza's voice is a sharp whisper from above.

Meg turns to call back.

'Barrels! I'm moving further in.'

'Hurry up.'

Meg steps forward. As far as she can see the crypt is a long room, although the light from her candle doesn't stretch to the far end which remains in darkness. To her right are barrels piled on top of each other. She smiles grimly, recognising the half ankers of gin that she carried from the boat, and which have given her shoulders the screaming pain of the last couple of days.

Next to them are more tubs, possibly with tea or brandy in them, and on the other side of the crypt are bales, wrapped tightly in oilskins that probably contained tobacco or maybe silks or lace.

Meg blinks and looks around. Here it all is, laid out before her. Probably the whole of the last haul from the coast.

'Meg!' Eliza's voice is sharp. 'Meg! There's someone coming in.'

Meg turns sharply at Eliza's voice.

'Coming,' she says, clutching the candle tightly in her hand and hurrying to the stairway where a rectangle of light is.

But before she can get there, she hears Eliza gasp. There is the sound of a scuffle, and the scrape of boots on stone and a sharp grunt from someone.

Then, before Meg can begin climbing the steps the trapdoor is lifted, with a screech of hinges, and swung over, gradually cutting the rectangle of light to a smaller and smaller shape until with a loud bang and puff of air that blows the candle out, it disappears altogether.

25

The slam of the wood as it settles into the frame goes through Meg like a sharp pain. In the enclosed space it is louder even than the musket shots the other night. She drops the useless candle as the dark envelops her like a cloak.

She frowns and puts a hand out to feel where she is. No chink of light comes from above. What is Eliza playing at? Is her friend trying to frighten her?

She strains to hear any sound from above but there is nothing. Either there is no-one in the church or the crypt is so well built as to allow no sound and light to filter in. She doesn't want to think about that. Eliza must still be there. Her only choice is to find the steps and hammer on the trap door.

Once she has determined the line of the wall it only takes her a few minutes to find the steps, although she bangs her shin on the bottom one before she stumbles up them.

Meg is not afraid of the dark but rarely has she been anywhere so black. The lack of light weighs on her and the thickness of it makes it difficult to breathe.

Eventually, on hands and knees, she manages to climb the stairs. She can feel where the roof changes from stone to wood. She pushes up on the trapdoor, but isn't surprised when it doesn't move. It was very heavy for two of them.

She tries pounding on it, but her hand produces only a feeble sound, albeit one that echoes round the stone chamber below her. The angle is awkward and very quickly Meg tires of the effort. She stops and tries putting her ear to the wood.

The surface is warm compared with the stone, but she can hear nothing from above.

'Eliza!' she shouts. 'Stop messing about and open the door.'

Even as she says it, she feels guilty. Eliza wouldn't have shut her down there, she is sure. But if she didn't, who did, and what has happened to Eliza?

In desperation she bangs and shouts until her throat is sore, and the edge of her hand is rough and bruised. She would do anything to get out. She chews her lip and wonders at what point someone will come. If she waits where she is she can grab at them as soon as the trapdoor is opened.

'I'll do anything!' she shouts. 'I'll never talk about the night business again. I'll never question Pa. Please! Let me out.'

She thumps on the wood and knocks and calls out again, but the energy is draining from her and eventually she collapses on the top step and weeps.

Meg isn't sure how long she sits there. It feels like hours but may only have been minutes. At last, as her thoughts scramble to understand what has happened, she wipes the sleeve of her frock across her eyes to dry them and sits up, crouching under the trapdoor.

'This is no good,' she tells herself. 'If Eliza was able, she'd open the door.'

She cocks her head but can hear

nothing from above. The dark is thick and impenetrable, pressing against her.

In the darkness the impossible becomes possible and Meg cannot tell what is real and what is not.

She breathes deeply but there doesn't seem to be enough air in the crypt. Does no air get down here without the trap-door open? She gasps, but the quicker she breathes the less air she seems to get.

She can feel her heart beating faster in her chest and hears the blood rush in her head. For a moment she feels woozy and thinks she might fall, so she shuffles down the steps on her backside until her feet reach the stone floor.

'You're making this worse,' she chides herself, putting a hand to her chest and making herself take a long slow breath.

As she breathes out again, she realises that the air is quite fresh and damp. And when she had had the candle, she hadn't seen any coffins or corpses.

'There is nothing to fear,' she mutters.

Meg decides to explore her prison as thoroughly as she can in the dark. She stands up and puts her arms out in front of her again, reaching to the right to find the wall. She knows there are tubs and half ankers, so she shuffles her feet along, feeling for them so she doesn't fall over.

It is slow going. Meg counts roughly a dozen tubs, stacked up in threes. There are more ankers, but then her foot finds space and her hand runs along blank, rough wall.

The crypt stretches another few feet and then her hand is stopped by a wall in front of her.

Is this the end of the crypt? Is this the size of her jail, Meg wonders, running her hand along the wall.

But instead of being a proper wall the stone she can feel is a stub and her hand touches nothing. There is an opening, like a doorway.

Meg's eyes widen in surprise. The candle hadn't lit this far into the crypt. It must have been in the shadows out of sight.

Keeping one hand on the wall she goes through the space and notices the air feels colder and the darkness appears slightly less black.

A little burst of hope blooms in Meg's chest. Could it be there is another way out?

She lurches forward and immediately trips over something, falling heavily on her knees and scraping the palms of her hands on the stone floor. Her eyes water but she stands up and wipes her hands down her frock.

This time she works her way forward more slowly, using her feet alternately in a sweeping motion, to make sure there is nothing in her way on the floor.

It is getting lighter, she feels sure. The blackness has changed to charcoal grey and as she goes further, she thinks she can even make out the outline of her hand in front of her.

Meg feels lighter as the darkness retreats but before she can get too excited, she hears a noise like dozens of footsteps marching together.

She freezes and instinctively drops down into a crouch, making herself smaller. Again, she forces herself not to panic and slows her heartbeat so she can listen carefully. The sound is constant and unchanging. She breathes deeply and stands.

One hand still on the wall she steps forward. She can see a faint light in the distance, maybe twenty or thirty yards ahead and the crypt has become narrower, more like a tunnel.

With increasing confidence Meg works her way down the tunnel. The sound of footsteps getting louder as she goes.

At last, the tunnel turns a sharp corner and there are steps up. Ahead she can see the graveyard through a metal grille and either side of her are shelves with metal doors on them.

She has come out in the graveyard in somebody's family vault, and judging by the size of it, Meg thinks, it must be Squire Padgett's.

She steps forward and it is then she realises what the sound is she heard. It is the rain drumming on the roof of the vault and on the leaves of the trees. From inside the tunnel, it sounds like marching feet. She takes a deep breath of fresh, wet air. It is good to see daylight, even if it is still pouring with rain.

Meg ignores the shelves around her, presumably filled with Padgett ancestors, and takes the metal grille in both hands and rattles it. It rocks but doesn't open. She moves closer and tries again and then notices the lock.

The metal grill scrapes in the metal frame as she wiggles it back and forward, screeching like the rabbit caught by the fox in the marshes. Meg freezes as a mob of crows takes off from the trees with harsh, raucous caws of indignation, but nobody comes, and the grill does not open.

Meg sags back against the shelving but immediately jumps forward, out of respect. So near but so far. She leans closer to the metal bars and peers through the gaps. There is nothing to see but trees, gravestones, and long grass. No-one is about. It is soaking wet and the ground, even this high on the slight mound above the village, is puddled and flooding.

A rush of alarm threatens to overtake her as Meg wonders what is happening at The Anchor. Has the dyke breached again? What will Pa and Nat do?

She rattles the grille but all it does is move slightly with a metal screech.

Meg sighs. She is no better off than she was inside the crypt. Nobody is likely to walk through the graveyard on a day like today, and it is doubtful anyone will go into the church. It's not a day for people to be out.

Tears prickle at the backs of Meg's eyes. She is about to sink down in defeat when she remembers the hair pins in her hair. She pulls one out roughly, ignoring the pain as several strands of hair come with it, straightens out the two prongs to a single length and pokes one end of it into the lock of the grille.

26

Meg twists the hair pin one way and then the other, trying to get it to catch on the lever inside the lock, but it proves frustrating and difficult.

After some half an hour of trying Meg is tired of stooping over the lock and a headache is beginning to pound in her temples.

She steps back into the vault and arches her back to get some relief when she hears sounds coming from outside. She peeks out through the grille, keeping to the shadows until she knows who it is, although she desperately hopes it is Eliza looking for her.

It's not Eliza, however. The figure, draped in a sailcloth coat that comes down well below his knees, and hat with a low brim to keep off the rain, is tall, broad and definitely male. Meg squints through the grille.

The figure walks stealthily along the

main path to the church porch. Meg watches as he avoids splashing as much as possible. Someone who doesn't want to be seen or heard, she thinks. Perhaps someone meeting Reverend Green or going to the crypt to move the contraband.

For a moment the wind blows the branches of the churchyard trees aloft, allowing more light in, and at the same moment the stranger looks up.

Meg jolts as she recognises Harry.

She instinctively moves closer to the grille and is about to shout out and wave when something stops her.

Where has Harry been? What has he been doing and why is he here now, when someone knows she is in the crypt and she and Eliza have been discovered finding the contraband?

As quietly as she can she steps back into the shadows again and lets Harry go on his way. Her heart is crying out to him, but for once she has thought this through.

Harry is still involved with Sissie. He

surely is just being nice to her while Nat is being looked after at The Anchor. He is against her finding out about Josiah and the night business, presumably because he is heavily involved in it and putting an end to it will affect him.

Meg presses her lips together. She can't expect rescue from that quarter, but she'll have to get out quickly because if people are going to go down in the crypt, they'll be expecting to find her there.

She wriggles her hairpin in the lock again and curses under her breath as it bends at a ninety-degree angle. For a moment she thinks it is not strong enough to work but the modification makes a difference and suddenly the lock snaps open and the grille door swings away from her.

Meg checks left and right. There is no one in sight and the crows have rearranged themselves in the trees and settled back down to their squabbling. She steps out in the rain, dragging her hood back over her head, although it is already soaking wet and serves more to disguise her than keep her dry.

Her feet are also damp as she cuts through the graveyard keeping to the grass to mask the sound of her footsteps. She should have rubbed her boots with goose grease, but who knew there would be this much rain before winter?

She makes a promise with herself that when she gets home, she will do both hers and Pa's boots and polish his coat and hat with linseed.

Meg works her way across to the porch and stands by the wooden door. The large curlicue hinges and rows of metal studs are supposed to keep the church safe from axemen and swordsmen but ironically, Meg thinks, not from smugglers.

She tries pressing her ear close to the warm wood, but she can hear nothing above the beating of the rain on the trees and ground outside. The weather is relentless, and she has no clue what is happening inside.

She takes a deep breath. She must go in and find Eliza. She grips the iron ring and twists it to lift the latch. The metal clanks but mercifully doesn't screech. Trying to keep the opening as narrow as possible, Meg slips inside and closes the door behind her.

It is immediately quieter inside the church and being out of the rain and wind is a relief. It appears darker than before. The candles that burn weakly in the sconces near the door do nothing but puddle light in a circle on the stone floor. Meg pauses and listens, her nerve endings tingling.

As her eyes become accustomed to the gloom, she can see a glow coming from the side aisle where the crypt is and as the pounding in her chest subsides, she can hear low voices and the scrape of things being moved.

Meg wonders what the best thing is to do. She could slip out again and try and find William Rufus and explain to him what she has seen. But she has no idea if he is still in the village or has ridden away to town or further along the coast. Although she saw him earlier, anyone in their right mind would surely be hidden away indoors in the inclement weather, especially if the dyke might be breached and the village might flood.

Then another sound startles her.

A low keening, muffled but frantic, seems to be coming from the side aisle.

Meg stands up taller, forgetting to flatten herself against the wall. She feels sure that it is Eliza.

She tiptoes across to the pews in front of her and, keeping down so her head doesn't protrude above the back of the benches, works her way along the wooden seats to the stone pillars which divide the main nave from the side aisles.

She stops at the end of the pew. A gap of a yard or so separates her from the side aisle. She sneaks up to the pillar and pushes herself against its cool, smooth surface. From here she can see, in the glow coming from the open trapdoor, a figure on the floor, writhing from side to side.

The dark cloak is twisted around the person, but Meg recognises Eliza's dress and her dark curls. Eliza has been trussed up like a chicken ready for market and a gag is across her mouth.

Meg freezes. Her immediate instinct is to run and help her friend, but caution makes her wait. Someone is down in the crypt and that someone has opened it up since Meg was down there. Do they know Meg was in there when they tied Eliza up?

Meg hovers, undecided, for a moment.

She peers round the pillar again. She will have to go and help Eliza.

She is about to step forward when a hand clutches her shoulder, and another is wrapped around her mouth preventing her from crying out. Meg's immediate reaction is beat at the hand, but her efforts are futile as she is pulled backwards against a body, bigger than her own and smelling of linseed and damp.

She tries to shake her captor off, but the grip simply tightens.

'Don't move.'

The words are hissed in her ear, barely above a whisper.

She recognises the voice. Harry.

Her heart beats faster as her legs threaten to give way beneath her.

She grits her teeth. She should have gone to find William Rufus. She was stupid. Now she can't help Eliza and both of them are caught.

27

Meg almost gags on the hand across her mouth. She'd wondered if Harry had been stringing her and Pa along until Nat was better, but she hadn't thought he'd go as far as to endanger Eliza's life. What is going to happen to her if she isn't rescued?

She tries to move the hand, but Harry is too strong for her, and she is like a mouse being held by a cat.

His voice whispers in her ear so quietly she's unsure she hears properly.

'If I move my hand do you promise not to shout out? Several of the gang are in the crypt moving the barrels. They'll be out like a ball from a musket if they hear us, and I don't like to think what they'll do.'

Meg takes a moment to process this information so busy is she with the thought that Harry is in with the smugglers but eventually she gives a slight nod of her head.

As soon as his hand is released, she spins around to confront him.

He's removed his hat and his hair flops over his face, the ends curling up with damp. His eyes are fixed on her face waiting for her to speak.

She gestures frantically towards her friend.

'Eliza,' she mouths.

Harry leans closer whispering in her ear, his voice tickling her like a gentle breeze.

'We'll do her more good by waiting to see what happens. She's uncomfortable but safe at the moment. If it changes, I'll —' He lets the sentence rest unfinished.

'Where are they taking it?' Meg whispers back.

Harry gives the slightest shrug.

'I don't know. I wasn't called. I came to the village looking for you. Nat said you'd been gone all day and it's pouring. The river is really high — almost at the top of the dyke.

'We told your pa, and he got us to move as much as we could upstairs or pile it out of the way in case the water breaks into The Anchor.'

Hearing Pa mention causes Meg's heart to trip. For a moment she's tempted to run from the church and hurry home to him to protect him from whatever is coming, but she allows Harry to pull her away from pillar along the pew towards the centre of the church.

They creep together to the shadows at the back of the church by the entrance door and Harry turns to talk to her, but before he can say anything there is a thud of wood on stone and looking across at the side aisle Meg can see the silhouette of somebody standing and arching their back.

'They're taking the stuff out of the crypt!' she hisses at Harry.

He wipes a hand across his brow.

'Aye. They'll be moving it up country.'

'Are you helping them?' Meg blurts out the words before she thinks about the consequences. If Harry is working with the smugglers still, he could be charged with taking care of her.

He turns and puts one hand on the side of her face.

'Do you want me to be?' he asks softly.

Meg glares at him.

'No!' The word shoots out of her mouth like water from a pipe. 'I've done my best to get Pa to stop working for them. It's trouble. The gang is bound to be caught one day and everyone will be hanged.

'Meanwhile, the long nights and the hard work of shifting stuff is near killing him.'

Harry nods.

'So how do we put a stop to it? Because if it's not stopped your Pa and me and everyone else will be reeled in again with threats to ourselves and our families.'

Meg swallows.

'Sergeant Rufus needs to see this,' she says slowly. 'But you need to be out of the way. And what about Eliza? We can't leave her there.'

Harry glances across at the side aisle.

Eliza is not visible from where they are standing but another man climbs out from the crypt and puts down a barrel with a boom that echoes round the church.

A thought occurs to Meg, and she turns to Harry, a scowl etched into her face like rune marks on stone.

'Where have you been these last few days? Why did you leave Nat?'

Harry pulls a face and flicks his hair out of his eyes.

'I had some business to take care of. One or two loose ends to tie up.'

Meg's eyes narrow.

'What? And you couldn't tell me or Nat you were going?'

'I didn't think it would take so long.'

Meg sees a flicker of indecision play across his face.

'But you still didn't think to mention to us that you were going? Nat was worried. I was worried. And with Pa sick, I had the Alehouse to run on my own.' She raises her hands and let them drop to her sides with a thump.

Harry immediately puts his finger to

his lips but there is more noise from the side aisle that covers any they might be making.

Another couple of barrels are thumped down on the stone floor and somebody coughs loudly and hawks on to the floor.

Harry grabs Meg's hand and pulls her further into the shadows.

'Meg,' he says urgently. 'You have to believe that I've been happier this last couple of weeks with you and your Pa than I have since our parents died.

'Well . . .' He pauses and considers. 'At least, I've been happier since Nat has been making a recovery. The Anchor is a happy, lively place and I can see why you love it so much and will do anything to protect it.

'When I say I had business to conclude, I did. I went to see Sissie. I told her when she appeared that things were over between us — they had never really started, the idea was mostly in her mind, but I had the feeling she didn't believe me because she didn't want to believe me.'

He takes a breath, glances across at the activity in the side aisle and continues.

'I had to make her see I meant it and the best way to do that was to move out of her mother's lodgings.

'I've packed up all that we own, which isn't much, given notice and moved out. Our stuff is in the Brewhouse at The Anchor. We have a couple of chairs that my father made but little else. Your Pa said it was fine to store it there.'

Meg leans back a little.

'Oh,' she says, not meeting his gaze. 'Oh.' But then she looks directly at him. 'You still could have said, rather than leave me wondering and doing all the work.'

Harry puts his hands up, palms forward.

'I could. I could, but I really didn't think it would take so long. Part of the reason is I had to get a cart, and then the road was getting so wet with the rain, it was difficult driving.'

Meg is somewhat mollified, although

she still can't help feeling that Harry should have told her what he was doing. Since he mentioned nothing, she has no idea if what he is saying is the whole truth.

'So, what do we do now?' she asks. 'I don't know how many barrels there were down there. A dozen or more? And some parcels.'

Harry nods.

'We need the excise men . . .'

'I can go and look,' Meg says. 'But I've no idea where they might be. They could have gone to Kirkstainton or anywhere. And if I don't find them, what happens?'

Harry shakes his head.

'I don't know where they are moving the stuff.'

'If I go, promise me one thing,' Meg says. 'You won't let them take Eliza anywhere. I want her released as soon as possible. No harm must come to her. She's not involved in any way.'

She looks up at Harry, her mouth set. He nods.

'I promise. I'll stay and watch them, and I won't let them take her anywhere. I don't know how many of them there are. Three, maybe. I can take them on.'

His voice is sharp and stiff, but Meg feels sure he is not as confident as he makes out.

Meg shakes her head.

'They'll fight to the death,' she says grimly. 'No heroics. I'll get the excise men. Just keep Eliza safe for me.'

'I will.'

Harry bends and cups her face in his hands and draws her to himself, kissing her full on the lips. Meg closes her eyes, inhaling his scent of outdoors, linseed, and masculinity.

She would like the moment to go on for ever, but another thump of goods being dumped on the church floor and another racking cough makes them jump apart.

Without a backwards glance, Meg slides over to the church door, twists the latch, and slips outside into the rain and the grey of evening.

28

Meg steps outside the church feeling as if she's dragging the shadow of the inside behind her. The vision of Eliza lying helpless and trussed niggles at her, and she quickly flicks her hair over her shoulder, raises her hood and sets off across the churchyard to the lych gate and the road beyond.

It is still raining, and heavy drips of water fall from the trees, from the church porch and the lych gate roof. Out in the road the puddles are so large they practically join up, and she must tiptoe along the visible patches of ground to find a route.

She has no idea where to find William Rufus. He normally appears at the most inopportune moments, but he doesn't live in the village and nor do his men, as far as she knows.

She walks towards the shop, her head down, concentrating on where she's putting her feet, rather like the wading birds who stride carefully through the shallows watching for fish and small crustaceans.

The road is deserted. No-one is out, which is not surprising considering the weather. Meg thinks she might try Mr Bracken first and ask after the excise men there.

The shop windows may be small, but Mr Bracken seems to know what goes on in the village. She is about to open the door when the splash of horse's hooves makes her turn.

For the first time ever the sight of William Rufus lifts her heart.

Quickly she retreats from the doorway and beckons to him.

If William is surprised, he doesn't show it. He dismounts next to Meg.

He raises his eyebrows as he waits for her to speak.

Meg looks up and down the road, but it is empty.

'There is contraband stored in the church, in the crypt. There are people in there moving it out now,' she whispers, checking all the time for anyone who might overhear them.

William shows no surprise and less interest than Meg expects.

'Well, aren't you interested?' she snaps.

'How do I know you are telling the truth?' He asks. 'Could it not be some trap?'

'What?' Meg is shocked. 'Why would I do that? You've be asking me for months about the smuggling along the coast.'

'Exactly,' he says. 'And you've decided to tell me today? What has changed? What is in it for you? And why should I believe you suddenly?'

She grits her teeth and breathes in deeply through her nose.

'I'm telling you because I thought you wanted to catch them. They trapped me down in the crypt and I had to find a way out through a vault in the church-yard and while I was doing that, they got hold of Eliza and tied her up.'

William's face contorts.

'They've taken a woman captive?'

'Yes,' Meg says. 'And if you don't hurry, they're going to move all the stuff and you'll never get them.'

The decision appears to churn about in William's head like a whirlpool before he snaps into action. He feels under his cloak for his side arm and gestures for Meg to lead the way.

They pick their way back down the road to the lych gate. William leads his horse inside and ties the reins round one of the inner supports.

Meg reaches the church door first and puts a finger to her lips. She twists the ring so the latch opens and slips through the narrowest gap she can. She is followed by William Rufus.

Immediately she is inside, Harry takes her arm.

'They are finished bringing the stuff out and are moving it to the back door,' he hisses.

Meg turns and sees William's expression has hardened.

'What's he doing here?' he whispers to Meg.

'He came looking for me when I didn't go home,' Meg says, hoping William's jealousies are not going to get in the way of him doing his job. 'He's just keeping an eye on Eliza while I came to find you.'

She's not sure William believes her but at that moment they hear a side door being opened and a barrel scraped across the ground.

'Stay here,' William hisses at them.

Meg grabs his arm before he can move away.

'There's only you,' she says. 'There are at least three of them and Eliza is floor over there, tied up.' She points to the side aisle.

'I have this,' William says, drawing his pistol. 'And the law.'

Meg almost rolls her eyes.

What would the smugglers worry about the law for? They've been illegally importing goods for years.

William strides off, round the end of the pews rather than squeezing through, his footsteps ringing on the stone floors.

Meg turns to Harry her face questioning.

But before they can do anything it is obvious the smugglers have heard him.

The Reverend Green appears from the steps of the crypt. There is light behind him, coming from below and his hair stands on end like a halo.

He puts his hands together in front of himself and stands with his legs slightly apart.

'What is the meaning of this?' he thunders using the sermon voice that has kept many a parishioner pinned to their seats. 'Why do you have a weapon drawn in God's house?'

'Why do you have barrels of contraband in the Lord's house?' William retorts.

Meg and Harry watch as he peers closer at the barrels.

'Not one of them duty paid,' he says.

Meg gestures to Harry and begins creeping along the pew, keeping down below the level of the seats so that the Reverend Green can't see her.

There are still at least two voices coming from the crypt.

William gestures at the Reverend Green with his pistol.

'Sit yourself down on the floor,' he hisses. 'And keep quiet.'

Then he leans over the steps of the crypt and shouts down.

'Come on up. You are surrounded.'

For a moment Meg thinks everything will be well. That the smugglers will come out as William asks. But there is an enormous amount of crashing from below and William fires his pistol into the crypt, the explosion ripping around the small space, ricocheting back and forth in waves.

Meg covers her ears and crouches down.

She hears footsteps and a scuffle and rises in time to see the Reverent Green leap forward and push William from behind, so he tumbles down the steps into the vault below ground.

The Reverend Green then turns and runs with a surprising turn of speed to the open side door and disappears.

Meg grabs Harry's arm.

'They're getting away,' she says. 'There's a way out of the crypt. It comes up in the churchyard at the stone vault. The grille is open because that's how I got out.'

'I'll go,' Harry says, vaulting over the pew and running to the main church door.

Meg hurries across to Eliza, whose eyes are wide and bright with fear. Meg can't tell if she is shaking in fear or trying to loosen her bindings.

Meg wrenches the gag down from her mouth and sets about untying the bonds that have forced her arms and legs back.

When Eliza is free Meg hugs her friend.

'M-m-meg,' Eliza stutters. 'Someone came up behind me and grabbed me and then they slammed the trapdoor shut.'

'It's all right,' Meg soothes her. 'I found a way out. Into the churchyard.'

Eliza shivers in her arms and then withdraws herself.

'Did I see Sergeant Rufus?' she asks.

Meg feels a stab of guilt.

What has happened him? He toppled down the steps into the crypt.

'Yes,' she says, jumping up. 'The Reverend Green hit him. I don't —'

She hurries the three steps to the crypt trapdoor and peers down. Eliza follows her.

Lying, sprawled on the steps below is William Rufus, and in the light from a couple of lanterns they can see something dark pooling beneath him.

'Quick,' Eliza says, gathering her skirts up for better movement and stepping down the first step. 'Check if he's breathing.'

Meg follows her and together they turn the excise man over. A long gash runs across his forehead where he has hit the edge of a step and there is blood on the back of his head, maybe from the fall, too.

'Help me sit him up,' Eliza puffs, working with her good arm and trying to prop the man up against her legs. Meg helps, hauling at William's shoulders so his head is at least level with his feet.

'Hold his head there,' Eliza says. 'I'll move his feet down, then maybe we can pull him out.'

Ten minutes later, when Harry returns, wet and hot and joins them by the trapdoor, they have managed to manoeuvre William up the steps and on to the floor of the church.

'Is he dead?' Harry asks, still out of breath.

'He's breathing,' Eliza says. 'But I don't know how badly he's hurt.'

'Did you see them?' Meg asks.

'Yes.' Harry bends over, gasping. 'But they got out of the vault and ran off. They had a head start on me and disappeared between the cottages. I don't know who they were or where they would have gone, not knowing the village well.'

Meg presses her lips together. She isn't sure if she believes him. Harry must know all the gang.

'Harry,' Eliza says. 'Can you help us move him? Can we take him to Mistress

Cooper? It's not far. She will know what to do, won't she?'

'I suppose so,' Meg says. She's never actually taken anyone sick to Mistress Cooper. 'I've no idea what she will make of him.'

'If we bundle him on to your oilskin, Harry, maybe we can carry it between us?'

They manage to load William Rufus on to the oilskin coat and Harry takes his head while Meg takes his feet and Eliza opens the church doors and provides a little assistance.

She hurries ahead to Mistress Cooper's cottage and by the time Harry and Meg get there the door is wide open, and the fire has been stoked up and Mistress Cooper is ready with water and clothes and is mixing a paste.

She gestures for Meg and Harry to put him on the mat by the fire and they lower him carefully down.

Meg stands back watching as Mistress Cooper bustles about.

'Will he make a recovery?' she asks,

biting her lip.

'I believe so,' Mistress Cooper says, as William stirs and moans. For a moment he opens his eyes and Meg feels sure he fixes his gaze on Harry. 'There is no need for you to stay. Your Pa is waiting for you. Eliza will remain.'

Meg arches an eyebrow at Eliza, who shrugs back. Meg grabs her friend's hand.

'I'll see you soon,' she says. 'Take care.'

Then she and Harry leave the cottage, shutting the door behind them and look out at the very wet road, as Meg wonders what they will find when they get to The Anchor.

29

They make their way back to The Anchor along the dyke path. The river is in full flood, fast flowing murky brown water rushing towards the sea. One boat is moored at the staithes, and it is pulling on the ropes making them creak and grind against the wooden piles.

The rigging flaps in the wind, metal pulleys and rings banging and tinkling like alternative church bells. In places, the river has topped the dyke, and the adventurous trickles of water have formed small lakes in the fields behind.

Fortunately, the heavy rains have abated and is now a constant drizzle, but the visibility is still poor, and they can't see more than halfway across the river.

Part way along the dyke, Meg realises she's forgotten her basket and the packet that Mistress Cooper gave her to make a tea for Pa. She wonders if she should turn back but when she mentions it to

Harry, he shakes his head.

'Your Pa was awake when I stopped this morning. I spoke to him,' he says. 'I'll warrant he's recovering. You'll be sick if you stay out in the wet here any longer.'

Meg dithers, undecided for a moment, but Harry persuades her towards home. She can feel her petticoats swishing around her ankles and her feet are damp in her boots. Rain has trickled inside the neckline of her frock and if she stops to think about it, she shivers.

They pass the warehouses and the ropewalk without seeing anybody and even the smithy appears shut, with extra wood placed across the doorway.

'Everybody is worried about the river,' Harry says.

Meg nods.

She's only seen it like this once before.

At last, The Anchor comes into view and Meg wants to run but her legs are heavy and tired. The wind from the sea is, if anything, more ferocious and tries to keep them back, but Harry wraps an arm round her and Meg leans into it and they push their way forward.

There is water all around the Ale house. The tide has been very high and coupled with the rain there are puddles all about, leaving The Anchor like an island.

Meg claps her hands to her face.

'No,' she murmurs, remembering the previous flood.

Harry pulls her round into the yard and opens the kitchen door.

Inside, the first thing Meg notices is that the floor is dry, before she is assaulted by Jip who jumps up wanting attention.

'Jip, Jip!' She bends and ruffles his ears and then looks around.

'Where's Pa?' she asks.

'We're up here!'

It's Nat's voice she hears coming from the first floor. Meg hangs her cloak on a hook and Harry removes his oilskin, retrieved from Mistress Cooper's, and they climb the stairs.

Nat's face is flushed, and he looks

pleased to see them.

'We've been watching the sea and the river,' he tells them. 'From your Pa's bedroom.'

Meg ducks under the door frame and into Pa's room. He is sitting up in bed and has a tankard of ale beside him, which he no doubt instructed Nat to fetch. There is the smell of smoke in the air, so he has also felt well enough for a pipe of tobacco.

Meg kneels beside Pa's bed.

'How are you feeling?' she asks.

Pa nods.

'Better,' he says, resting his hand on her arm. 'Young Nat has been minding me.'

'I'm sorry,' Meg says. 'I went to Mistress Cooper to get something for you and then —' She raises her hands helplessly and looks at Harry.

Pa turns and looks at him, too.

'There was an incident,' Harry says carefully. 'William Rufus found the Reverend Green had stored contraband in the crypt at the church.'

Pa's eyes flicker from Harry to Meg and back.

Meg is grateful that Harry is keeping her role in this out of it.

'Rufus was hurt. We took him to Mistress Cooper and Reverend Green and the others escaped, but now Rufus will be wise to them.'

Pa strokes his chin which is stubbly and makes a scratchy sound.

'So, Josiah is the Reverend Green?' Pa asks carefully, then his forehead puckered. 'But his name is not Josiah, is it?'

'I don't believe so, Pa,' Meg says. 'We're not sure if he was directing operations or if there is someone above him. I suppose William Rufus will . . .' She stopped and bit her lip. 'Will investigate when he is well.'

'So, no more night business for us?' Pa asks in a low voice, looking between Meg and Harry.

Harry shakes his head.

'It would seem not. I don't know if the contraband was always hidden at the church, but that place is certainly discovered and so is the Reverend Green.'

Meg clenches her fists at the thought of that man who stood each Sunday, extolling them to be righteous citizens, running a smuggling gang on the side and controlling men as he saw fit.

Pa takes her hands in his.

'It's fine, Meggie. We'll be fine. We'll manage without the money.'

Meg glances up at Pa. He's misunderstood her anger. It's not the money she is cross about. She will be more than relieved to have Pa safe home at nights, and she knows they will manage.

It's that he would expect Pa and the others to work for him until their death and they had no choice in the matter. She sighs.

But before the conversation can continue Nat butts in.

'Meg, I moved the goat into the Brewhouse as the field was flooding.'

Meg looks up, alarmed.

She hasn't thought about The Anchor itself, she was so worried about Pa.

She smiles at him.

'Thank you,' she says, getting up. 'Right, let's go and see where everything is.'

Meg and Harry check the building. Plenty of rain has come through the roof and Nat's pallet is wet. It is decided he and Harry will sleep by the fire in the kitchen tonight. But no water is in the Ale house itself, and although the yard is flooded, the Brewhouse and the out-houses remain dry.

Meg splashes out and checks on the chickens who are annoyed not to be let out, but their field is mostly under water. She gives them some food and shuts them back up as night comes rolling in. The garden, she notices, has also taken a pounding and will need work.

Meg stands in the kitchen and rotates her shoulders. She is so tired she is almost asleep on her feet.

'Get yourself to bed,' Harry urges. 'I'll sort out myself and Nat. They'll be no company this evening. People will know it's flooding, and no-one is working on the staithes.'

Meg knows what he says is right. It's

unlikely they'll have customers tonight and if they are looking for a meal, they would be unlucky anyway as she hasn't cooked. But she can't go to bed without getting the remains of yesterday's bread and cheese that she'd wrapped in waxed paper and making a picnic to take up to Pa.

They all sit in Pa's room, and Jip scampers from one to the other of them, excited to find them at floor level.

When Meg can keep her eyes open no longer, Harry gently takes the wooden platter from her hands and puts it down, then steers her into her own room sits her down on her bed and removes her boots.

Meg doesn't even bother to remove her clothes but swings her legs up and lies down. She feels a blanket drawn over her and immediately sinks into blackness.

Sometime later Meg rises to consciousness and can hear a conversation coming from Pa's room. She is not particularly concerned and would like to drift back to sleep, but a mention of her name jerks her fully awake.

'You'll have to ask her yourself,' Pa is saying. 'But I've no objections. I could certainly do with a hand around here and Nat seems keen to learn about the brewing.'

A male voice answers him but is too quiet for Meg to hear.

'She has a mind of her own, my daughter,' Pa says. 'But she's a good girl. She's worked hard since her Ma died. It's not been the best life for her.'

Again, there is more muttering in reply that Meg doesn't catch and then a guffaw of laughter from her father.

Meg's expressions hardens but she doesn't know what they are laughing about, and she can't raise the energy to get up and creep nearer to listen. She's done enough creeping around recently. Enough for a lifetime.

A thought flitters around in her head, butterfly-like, not settling. She concentrates, trying to catch hold of it, but it skitters just out of reach.

Was Pa giving Harry his blessing to stay here and live with them? A warm feeling spreads through her. Then the butterfly flutters back.

William Rufus saw Harry in the church and at Mistress Cooper's cottage. He might have been groggy, but she saw the flash of recognition in his eyes.

Please, she thinks, please don't come for Harry. He's not the one you want . . .

30

In the morning Meg stretches luxuri- ously in her bed before remembering the snatches of conversation she heard the previous evening and the thought of William Rufus demanding revenge that she went to sleep with.

She jumps up with a start and when she opens the shutters, she finds the storm has blown itself out. The sea is a soft velvety silver and above are bright blue skies.

She flings open her bedroom window to the day to air the room, dresses in an old petticoat and her best dress before taking yesterday's clothes downstairs to clean.

She starts when she finds Nat and Harry curled up on the floor in front of the cold fire, but Jip is delighted to find them at his level and wakes them with licks and kisses.

'I'll fetch some more logs,' Meg says

when they look up at her resentfully.

When she comes back in, dragging a full log basket, Nat has curled up on a chair, but Harry has gone to the pump and is washing himself down.

'Did William Rufus see you yesterday?' Meg asks him in a low voice.

Harry looks at her.

'Aye, in the church.'

'Will he think you were involved with the smuggling?' Meg asks.

Harry scratches his head and smiles at her.

'Well, I would hope you would tell him the truth,' he says.

'Of course I will,' Meg says. 'But that doesn't mean he'll believe me. He has his own way of thinking and once an idea has taken hold, there is not much that will shake it free.'

A frown crosses Harry's face.

'Perhaps we should be cautious, but I'm guessing he'll be laid up for a few days.'

Meg makes breakfast and is relieved when Pa gets up and comes downstairs, although he is still wheezing. He eats a little gruel with plenty of honey and mutters he needs to get out to the Brewhouse.

Nat volunteers to go and help him and light the fires and carry things he needs.

Pa ruffles his hair and calls him a good lad.

Harry and Meg put the goat back in the field and let the chickens out. There are still puddles about and everything looks windswept. Harry spends time righting parts of the fence around the garden that have blown down.

'This should have a proper bank around it,' he says. 'To protect it if the water rises again. You don't want the garden covered by salt water.'

Meg shrugs.

'There's plenty of spray that gets on it already,' she says.

'But better a bank to protect it more,' he says.

''Tis too much work for Pa,' Meg tells him.

Harry looks thoughtful.

'Meg —' he begins.

'Harry —' Meg says at the same time.

'You first.' She folds her arms over her chest.

'Come for a walk along the shore,' Harry says. 'Bring that daft dog.'

Meg whistles for Jip who comes bounding up. The storm has brought extra seaweed and branches and wood up the beach, much higher than it would normally be. While Meg throws a stick for Jip, Harry pulls out good planks and makes a pile.

'This will all be fine for repairing The Anchor,' he says.

Meg gives him a sideways look.

'Meg,' he says, his voice low and solemn. 'I'm sorry I disappeared. I told you; I had something to deal with and now it's done.'

'Are you going to leave us?'

Harry's eyebrows draw together.

'No.' He shakes his head. 'Well, not if you don't want me to. That's what I was doing. I went,' Harry says slowly and carefully, 'to straighten out my relationship with Sissie. She is beautiful, yes, but . . . my heart does not lie with her.'

He stares at Meg and heat spreads through her. His intense grey eyes are the colour of the estuary in the early morning before dawn has fully cracked through the night mist.

His face is paler that when she first saw him. Too much time inside, she thinks idly to herself.

Still, Meg folds her arms across her chest.

'How can I trust you?' she said. 'You seem very free with your affections.'

Harry staggers back, his hand on his heart.

'Oof!' he says. 'That cut. There was nothing between Sissie and I. Nothing confirmed. Nat and I lodged with her ma, and I think there was a presumption that we might stay.

'I know Nat is much happier here. He likes your Pa very much. He loves the estuary. And . . .' He pauses. 'If I am happy, he is happy too. If you doubt my intentions, can I ask, may I speak to your Pa about marriage?'

Blood rushes to Meg's head and she staggers slightly.

Harry leaps forward to steady her.

'Please say yes,' he says. 'I'd like nothing more than to spend the rest of my life with you.'

Meg takes a couple of deep calming breaths and fiddles with the edge of her shawl.

'I think I would like that very much,' she says as Harry's face breaks into a huge grin that dimples his cheeks and creases the skin round his eyes.

'Yes!' He pulls her forward and lifts her under the arms, swinging her round so her feet leave the ground.

When he sets her down, Meg's world spins, but she is aware of the sound of clapping coming from the Alehouse.

She turns and looks back. Pa and Nat are clapping and waving.

★   ★   ★

It is three days before Meg hears from Eliza, three days where she frets about what might happen to Harry. Once or twice, she's thought of going into the village to see William Rufus at Mistress Cooper's, but she is busy catching up in the Alehouse, making bread, stews, cleaning and sweeping.

Nat has been good with her father, working as an assistant to him, and Harry has cleaned around the yard and tidied the garden and started work on repairing the roof now that Amos has delivered some straw.

The message, when it comes, makes Meg raise her eyebrows. William is awake but still not well and has returned to his house in town, taking Eliza and her mother with him to look after him.

According to Eliza the word is out, and the excise men are after the Reverend Green. Some contraband was collected from the church, but much had already been spirited away by wily villagers.

A few days later, as Pa and Nat are in the Brewhouse and Harry is working on the roof of The Anchor, Meg hears horse's hooves coming along the dyke.

She hurries out to the yard.

'Harry,' she hisses.

Harry looks down and Meg jerks a thumb over her shoulder.

'I'll have to face him sometime, Meg,' Harry says. 'Better to get it over with.'

Meg swallows. She doesn't feel as nonchalant as Harry appears. She knows William Rufus has a spiteful streak. It would be just like him to round up Harry and Pa as members of the gang.

However, today the man is on his own. He dismounts and ties his horse to the fence and comes into the yard.

'Good afternoon, Meg,' he says.

'Good afternoon, Sergeant Rufus,' Meg replies. 'I hope you're feeling somewhat better.'

William Rufus removes his hat and Meg can see a bandage round his forehead.

'I am, thank you,' he says. 'Eliza tells me I have you and,' he glances up at the roof, 'your cousin to thank for that.

Without your help I could have been left on the steps of the crypt.'

'I hope you don't think we would do that,' Meg says.

'Yes, well, perhaps not,' William Rufus admits.

'More important,' Meg says. 'Have you found the Reverend Green? He seems to have been running this smuggling ring that you've been after.'

'Yes,' William Rufus says. 'That's what I came to tell you. He is locked up and will appear at the assizes next week.

'He appears to have run the gang himself, but he is giving up no names and we are no nearer to finding those who were helping him in the crypt.'

Meg says nothing. The men will have disappeared as easily as the contraband, and the village won't give them up. She is sure William knows this, too, but no doubt he lives in hope of getting the whole gang.

'At least you have the leader,' Meg says.

'I was hoping to catch them all,' William Rufus says, rubbing his chin. 'But I suppose I shall have to be content with stopping the activities along this part of the coast, at least.'

Meg nods and William Rufus puts his hat back on and mounts his horse.

'Thank you again,' he says and raises his hand as he leaves.

As soon as he's gone Pa and Nat come out of the Brewhouse.

'And that's all?' Pa asks. 'Seems some of the wind has gone out of him.'

'Must have been the fall down the steps,' Harry says.

But Meg has an idea that someone else may have mellowed him a little.

★ ★ ★

Two years later Meg is walking along the dyke again. She has been to visit Eliza in town, which involves a cart ride from the village. Eliza is blissfully happy. William has provided the promised house, and she has a girl who comes in and helps every day.

Her ma lives with them, too, which is

useful now that Eliza and William have baby Isaac, a child with more clothes than Meg can imagine.

Reverend Green was hanged for his nefarious activities three months after Meg got out of the crypt, and there is a new minister at the church. He married Harry and Meg soon after Eliza and William's wedding.

Meg knows the night business hasn't gone. While the king is raising taxes for his wars and pricing goods out of folk's reach it will continue, but the gangs work further along the coast and Pa and Harry are no longer involved.

Meg must ignore it when the odd barrel of Holland's gin or brandy appears in the Brewhouse. Everyone is involved in the business somehow, except perhaps William Rufus, whose pursuit of the smuggling gangs has moved, too.

Meg waves at the men at work at the staithes. Sailors are fixing the sails and rigging of the boats as the longshoremen unload goods and transfer them to carts, the horses and donkeys waiting patiently.

The Anchor comes into view beyond, and as always, Meg blinks. Harry has built an extension to one side. She now has a bigger kitchen and a store for food and utensils. Upstairs they have another room too, and all the shutters fit, and the roof has been freshly thatched.

It seems Pa had a small store of coins he earned but hadn't spent. A son-in-law to take over the business was all the incentive he needed for a little investment.

Meg turns the corner into the yard behind the Ale house. Jip is lying against the wall in the sunshine. She bends down and scratches him behind his greying ears. He doesn't go far these days, but when Nat is home from the fishing boats, he tries to chase the sticks Nat throws for him.

'Meg! Come and see,' Harry calls.

He stands in the doorway of one of the outhouses that he uses as a workshop. Stacked neatly outside are planks of wood he's collected from along the beach.

Meg steps inside the shed, waiting for a moment for her eyes to adjust to the dark.

On the floor, is a wooden cradle on rockers, with spindles at each corner to move it. Harry has polished the wood, so it gleams.

'Thought it was time,' Harry says.

Meg cradles her stomach. There's nothing to show, but she's felt her body changing over these last few weeks.

'How did you know?' she asks.

'We are one.' Harry grins.

'Soon we'll be three,' she says.

'All the better,' Harry says and leans down to kiss her, his mouth tasting of salt and sea and love.

We do hope that you have enjoyed reading this large print book.

Did you know that all of our titles are available for purchase?

We publish a wide range of high quality large print books including:
Romances, Mysteries, Classics
General Fiction
Non Fiction and Westerns

Special interest titles available in large print are:
The Little Oxford Dictionary
Music Book, Song Book
Hymn Book, Service Book

Also available from us courtesy of Oxford University Press:
Young Readers' Dictionary
(large print edition)
Young Readers' Thesaurus
(large print edition)

For further information or a free brochure, please contact us at:
Ulverscroft Large Print Books Ltd.,
The Green, Bradgate Road, Anstey,
Leicester, LE7 7FU, England.
Tel: (00 44) 0116 236 4325
Fax: (00 44) 0116 234 0205

Other titles in the
Linford Romance Library:

CHRISTMAS AT SANDY BAY

Audrey Mary Brooks

December, 1957. Melody Bright and boyfriend Trevor are looking forward to a festive season together as entertainers at Trimbles Holiday Camp. With missing reindeer, unreliable heating, howling dogs, and falling scenery, disaster seems to follow disaster. Even the camp compère is bickering constantly with the star turn and neglecting his duties. Can the entertainment team pull together by Christmas Day to impress a mystery guest and make Sandy Bay 'Trimbles Christmas Holiday Camp of the Year'?

TICKET TO ROMANCE

Philippa Carey

At Paddington Station, Sir Martin Locke comes across a young woman whose purse, including her money and her train ticket, has been stolen. Feeling he cannot just walk on by, he purchases his new acquaintance — Miss Veronica Douglas — a fresh ticket and luncheon. The two spend the journey in companiable conversation. But the line becomes blocked by snow, and neither can reach their destination as expected. Martin feels committed to Veronica's rescue, so what is he going to do?

A CHRISTMAS KISS

Alan C. Williams

Cindy Powers has a special gift: sometimes she can see into the past or the future. One such vision shows her a picture of Christmas years before, with someone who was very special to her — before it all went wrong between them. But why is it coming back to haunt her now?